"Bliss," Dutton pleaded, "I can't kiss you, because if I do—"

She laced her fingers around his neck and leaned closer to him. Dutton groaned. He ached for her, burned for her like the fire in the hearth. "Bliss, please listen to me."

"No. This time, please, listen to me," she said, her mouth close to his lips. "I'm just Bliss, your sweet Bliss. I'm your Christmas angel, only yours. There's no world beyond this room, Dutton. No questions, no answers, only the two of us with our beautiful Christmas tree and the warmth of the fire. It's our night, a magical night." She drew a shuddering breath. "I want you, Dutton McHugh, and I'll never regret it, never."

Dutton pulled her close to him, tasted her lips as if he'd never touched them before. She wanted him. Bliss wanted him. His Christmas miracle. . . .

WHAT ARE *LOVESWEPT* ROMANCES?

They are stories of true romance and touching emotion. We believe those two very important ingredients are constants in our highly sensual and very believable stories in the *LOVESWEPT* line. Our goal is to give you, the reader, stories of consistently high quality that may sometimes make you laugh, sometimes make you cry, but are always fresh and creative and contain many delightful surprises within their pages.

Most romance fans read an enormous number of books. Those they truly love, they keep. Others may be traded with friends and soon forgotten. We hope that each *LOVESWEPT* romance will be a treasure—a "keeper." We will always try to publish

LOVE STORIES YOU'LL NEVER FORGET
BY AUTHORS YOU'LL ALWAYS REMEMBER

The Editors

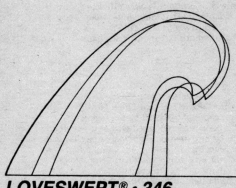

LOVESWEPT® • 346

Joan Elliott Pickart
Sweet Bliss

 BANTAM BOOKS
NEW YORK • TORONTO • LONDON • SYDNEY • AUCKLAND

SWEET BLISS

A Bantam Book / August 1989

If you would be interested in receiving protective vinyl
covers for your Loveswept books, please write to this address
for information:

Loveswept
Bantam Books
P.O. Box 985
Hicksville, NY 11802

ISBN 0-553-22016-0

Published simultaneously in the United States and Canada

Bantam Books are published by Bantam Books, a division
of Bantam Doubleday Dell Publishing Group, Inc. Its trademark, consisting of the words "Bantam Books" and the
portrayal of a rooster, is Registered in U.S. Patent and
Trademark Office and in other countries. Marca Registrada.
Bantam Books, 666 Fifth Avenue, New York, New York 10103.

For
Elaine and Bob
Rachael and David
New family, new friends

One

So, Bliss Barton thought dully, *this* was a hangover.

She shifted on the bed and instantly realized that had been a mistake as pain rocketed through her head. She was not, she decided, going to open her eyes or try to move again. Death could simply claim her while she lay straight as a pencil, and that would be that.

Maybe she'd moan, she thought. The way she felt, she deserved to moan . . . a lot. Everything hurt. Not just her head, but everything, including her nose, teeth, stomach, and, yes, even her hair. Sunlight was beating against her eyelids, and that was extremely rude because her eyelids hurt. Oh, where was the grim reaper when a person needed him?

It had, she admitted, been quite a party. Not that she remembered much after the seventh or eighth champagne toast made to her brother and his bride-to-be. Steve and Mandy had looked so happy, so in love, and Bliss had lifted her glass time and again like a trouper. She, who usually made one drink last an entire evening, had guzzled the delicious, bubbly wine.

Well, she rationalized, it wasn't every day of the week that one's older brother set the date to marry the woman of his heart. And the party had been in Bliss's apartment, so she hadn't had to worry about driving in her socially unacceptable condition. The truth of the matter was, she didn't even remember how she'd gotten into bed.

Did one's dying in one's own bed, she wondered, have the same pizzazz as a cowboy's croaking with his boots on? Was she at least going to check out with a little class? Oh, dear heaven, her poor, aching self.

Bliss moaned.

She moaned because she'd earned the right, and because maybe there was an outside chance that it would somehow make her feel better. It didn't, but she moaned again anyway.

"No joke," a deep voice mumbled.

Bliss stiffened so quickly that she jerked on the bed. Her eyes flew open, and she turned her head sharply. In wide-eyed, pain-ridden horror she stared at the please-don't-let-this-be-true scene before her.

Stretched out next to her on the double bed was a man. A half-naked man, clad only in gray slacks, lying on his back. One large hand was splayed on his flat, bare stomach, while his other arm lay next to her. His eyes were closed, dark lashes fanning on lean cheeks, and a dark stubble of beard covered a square jaw.

She was looking at his profile, could see his high forehead, straight nose, the hint of what would probably be nicely shaped lips. His hair was a thick, tousled black mass. Wide shoulders matched his beautifully muscled arms and chest, and he was tall, his bare feet reaching nearly to the end of the bed.

He was, without a doubt, Bliss mused, one fantastic hunk of the male species.

But what was he doing in her bed?

Stay calm, Bliss told herself. She always stayed calm. She was known for her calmness. She prided herself on the fact that when everyone around her lost it, she maintained her proper demeanor and, for Pete's sake, stayed calm!

A funny little noise escaped from her lips. She knew it was hysteria waiting to break loose in the form of an ear-splitting scream. She definitely was *not* calm.

There was a half-naked man in her bed!

She'd never seen him before in her life!

She had no idea how he'd gotten there!

She screamed.

The man shot up to a sitting position. Bliss's body went rigid, and she clamped her mouth closed before another scream could erupt. The man cradled his head in both hands and groaned, a deep noise that seemed to come all the way from the bottom of his big, bare feet. He flopped back against the pillow with a thud, his hands still pressed to his head, his eyes closed.

"For cripes sake," he said gruffly, "have mercy. Don't do that again."

Bliss scrambled out from beneath the blankets, ignoring the throbbing pain in her head and eyes. Kneeling on the bed, she noted absently that she was wearing her purple football jersey nightshirt with the number ten in white on the front. She pressed one hand to her forehead as a wave of dizziness assaulted her, then straightened.

"Hey," she said, aware that her voice was shaking, "who in the blue blazes are you, and what are you doing in my bed? And how did you get here? And I'll scream if I darn well please, mister, because this is my bedroom and you don't belong in it. Now haul your big carcass up and out of here, or I'll scream loud enough to bring the marines running. Got that?"

He dropped his hands to his chest, slowly turned his head, and peered at her with one, half-opened eye. "Huh?'"

Oh, he really was gorgeous, Bliss thought. She could see all of his face now, and he was something, stubbly beard, messy hair, and all. Even in his disheveled state he oozed power and masculinity, each part of him more magnificent than the last. That, however, did not erase the fact that she had no idea who he was, nor that he had no business whatsoever being in her bed.

"Get out of my bed!" she shouted.

"Oh, damn," he said, squeezing his eyes closed, "would you quit yelling? I'm dying here, Bliss. The least you can do is let me go to my maker in peace."

Bliss? she thought frantically. He knew who she was? Why didn't she know who *he* was? He felt, apparently, as rotten as she did, which meant he'd tipped too many at the party too. Still she didn't remember meeting him, or even seeing him. Oh, Lord, this was mortifying. Nothing like this had ever happened to her in her twenty-five years. She led a quiet, orderly, *calm* life. Bliss Barton didn't wake up with a hangover and a strange man in her bed. Bliss Barton didn't wake up with *any* man in her bed, thank you very much. She didn't give wild parties, either.

Well, she thought dryly, when she blew it, she didn't mess around. She'd hosted the bash of the year, gotten blitzed for the first time in her life, and was suffering pain and agony from her overindulgence. And there was a half-naked stranger in her bed.

The tricky part now, Bliss decided, massaging her temples, was to come out of this fiasco with at least a shred of her dignity intact. Was she calm? Yes, she'd gotten it together, was back in control and as calm as a summer breeze. She hoped.

"Well," she said, striving for a lightness to her voice, but not quite pulling it off, "I've heard of leftovers from a party, but I always thought that meant stuff you could put into Tupperware." She paused. "Small joke there."

"Mmm," the man said.

"But the party is long over, so it's rise and shine time, everybody goes home. Right? Absolutely."

"Mmm."

"I'm going to trot my little self into the shower, and when I come out, you'll be gone, poof, disappeared, never to be seen again. Here I go, into the shower."

"Bliss, would you please, *please*, be quiet?"

"That does it." She spun around and slid off the bed, weaving unsteadily for a moment when she stood. She flattened her hands on the top of her head with the hope of keeping it attached to the rest of her body and glared at the inert form on the bed. "You have three seconds to get up and out of here, buster, or I'm calling the police. If you think I'm kidding, just try me. Oh, and another thing. How is it that you know my name, when I don't have the foggiest notion who you are? Answer me that."

The man turned his head and opened both eyes, revealing irises such a deep shade of brown, they were nearly black, the pupils hardly discernible.

What beautiful eyes, she thought, and they were

surrounded by such long dark lashes. He really was something. Oh, forget it. Enough was enough.

"I'm Dutton McHugh," he said, his voice deep and rumbly. "Your brother, Steve, introduced us at the party last night."

And she was Bliss, Dutton mused, with the bright blue eyes and riot of auburn curls that fell to her shoulders. Bliss Barton, a slender woman of average height with delicate, lovely features and very sensuous lips. She'd looked terrific the night before in an emerald green jumpsuit that accentuated her tiny waist and small, but enticing, breasts.

Now she stood there in a football jersey, her hands on top of her head. The jersey was hiked up to reveal shapely thighs, and was pulled tightly over her pert breasts. She looked like a storm about to happen, and he could feel a sensual heat gathering low and heavy in his body. There should be nothing appealing about someone suffering from an obvious hangover, he thought, but Bliss was sensational. And she didn't even remember meeting him. Damn.

"I got here late," he said, "because my plane was delayed. They stack planes up like a tower of building blocks above your Denver airport. Anyway, by the time I arrived, the party was in full swing. And, apparently"—he smiled—"so were you, since you don't remember meeting me. I just thought you were an extremely happy person."

Great, Bliss thought. On top of everything else, Mr. Dutton McHugh had a smile that could melt icebergs. To some other woman, she supposed, finding a surprise package like Dutton in her bed would seem like an early Christmas present. To Bliss this was the worst nightmare of her life. That wasn't to say Dutton wasn't the most astonishingly handsome man she'd ever feasted her eyes on, but she just didn't do things like this.

And she was still doing it, she thought dismally. Dutton was still in her bed, and she hadn't made one iota of progress toward removing him from the premises. Oh, her aching head.

"Oh, my aching head," she said, then tossed in a moan for good measure. She dropped her hands to plant them on her hips. "Look, Mr. McHugh . . ."

"Dutton." He sat up slowly, grimacing against the pain, then draped his hands over drawn up knees. "Call me Dutton, and I'll call you Bliss. Your brother and I go way back. I'm practically like family."

Family? he mentally repeated. The way his body was reacting to Miss Bliss Barton did not even hint of a brotherly relationship. Did she have any idea how totally enchanting she looked all sleepy and rumpled, her hair a tangle of auburn curls beckoning to his fingers to weave through them? No, he didn't think she did know. He'd like to leap across the bed, haul her into his arms, and—

"Dutton," she said firmly, "you and Steve may be good old buddies, but I don't know you from Adam. Even if I did, your being in my bed uninvited simply isn't acceptable."

"So, invite me," he said, flashing her a dazzling smile. She glowered at him. "Forget I said that. Look, nothing happened here. I don't usually pass out at parties, Bliss. I was dead tired, hadn't had much to eat, and"—he shrugged—"the champagne really hit me and I conked out, I guess."

"Do you think *I* do this on a regular basis?" she asked, her voice rising. "Oh-h-h, my head. I've never been sloshed in my life. Where was Steve? How dare he leave a strange man in my bed."

"I'm not strange, I'm perfectly normal. I am, in fact, going to be best man at the wedding. Steve and I were in the navy together years ago and have kept in touch ever since. He's visited me in San Francisco many times."

"You're *that* good old buddy? Yes, now that I think about it, your name is vaguely familiar, connected, I believe, with stories of my brother's rowdy escapades."

"That was during my reckless youth." He smiled again. "Steve and I are pillars of the community now."

"Steve has settled down a tad since meeting and falling in love with Mandy. She's had a somewhat steadying effect on him at least."

"Oh, really? Maybe that's what I need, Bliss. A good woman to take me in hand, keep me on the straight and narrow, give purpose and direction to my life, and—"

"Oh, just zip it, McHugh." Bliss spun around, immediately clamped one hand on her forehead, and started across the room. "I'm taking my shower now." She yanked open a dresser drawer and grabbed some clothes with her free hand. "When I come out, be gone, vanished." She entered the bathroom and closed the door with a decisive click.

"But I just got here, sweet Bliss," Dutton said, grinning at the bathroom door.

In the shower, Bliss closed her eyes as the hot water streamed over her like a comforting blanket. Dutton McHugh, she mused. Yes, she definitely remembered that name now from the stories Steve had told. Or, closer to the truth, stories she'd overheard Steve telling their father, punctuated with man-to-man chuckles. Steve and Dutton had been a rowdy, womanizing pair as they'd strutted their stuff in their spiffy navy uniforms. Steve was finally settling down a little at age thirty-two, but only because Mandy was in his life now.

Bliss shampooed her hair and sighed in relief as some of the pain in her head and eyes began to subside. Had Dutton McHugh settled down? Despite his claiming to be a "pillar of the community," was he still a rowdy womanizer?

He certainly hadn't seemed very distressed to wake up with someone he'd been introduced to the night before. With his looks, and build, and gift for dishing out charming blarney, he no doubt had women trailing after him like panting puppies. He needed a good woman to keep him on the straight and narrow? Ha! He probably needed a warden to keep him out of trouble.

"Not my type," Bliss said aloud, nearly swallowing a mouthful of water. "Definitely not my type."

She turned off the water and reached for a towel as she stepped out of the shower. No, he wasn't her type, but the rest of the Bartons—Steve, her mother and father—would welcome Dutton McHugh with open arms. She could well remember her father laughing with delight at Steve's stories, telling his son that he was a chip off the old block. If Dutton still possessed his happy-go-lucky attitude of days past, he'd fit right into the Barton clan.

But she didn't fit in.

Bliss sighed as she toweled her hair. She was odd man out, she knew, and always had been. She was too cautious, too set in her ways, to qualify as a true-blue Barton. Oh, they all loved her, and she worshiped her family, but she'd always felt separated from them, one step over and back from their attitudes and outlooks.

She dressed in jeans and a green sweater, then pulled a brush through her tangled, damp hair. Even Mandy, she'd noticed, had that telltale gleam in her eye that said she was ready for adventure. Mandy had certainly curbed some of Steve's wilder impulses, but the pair was by no means sedate. They were presently camping out in sleeping bags in an old house they'd purchased and were renovating from top to bottom. Definitely not Bliss's cup of tea.

And now here was Dutton McHugh, she thought, Steve's best friend, yet another person who would show just how much she did *not* fit the Barton mold. To her, Dutton was as welcome as a toothache. And he certainly wasn't welcome in her bed.

She yanked open the bathroom door, stopped, blinked, then walked slowly into the bedroom, her gaze riveted to the bed.

He was gone. Dutton was gone. Well, of course, he was, she told herself. She'd given very precise orders regarding his leaving immediately. And, no, for crying out loud, that was not a flicker of disappointment she felt. What an absurd thought. Dutton was gone, and good riddance to him. During his stay in Denver, she was definitely keeping out of his way. As Steve's best friend, Dutton was automatically not her type. Dutton was a Barton clone, and Bliss was a Barton in name only.

Bliss wrinkled her nose. Coffee? Did she actually smell the aroma of freshly brewed, life-giving coffee? What a strange thing a hangover was. She'd had the fleeting idea that the remaining traces of her headache could be cured by two aspirin with matching mugs of steaming coffee, and her subconscious was now supplying the smell of what she was longing for. Weird.

She shoved her feet into the fuzzy red and green striped slippers Steve had given her for Christmas the previous year and shuffled out of the bedroom. Walking with a firm step, she'd discovered as she'd left the bathroom, was not a kind thing to do to her tender head.

At the doorway to the kitchen, Bliss stopped, looked, and screamed.

Dutton spun around and flattened himself against the counter, glaring at Bliss. "Would you quit doing that? My head isn't up to enduring air raid sirens this morning, Bliss."

She stomped into the kitchen, her head protesting the sudden and turbulent motion. "What are you doing in here? You're supposed to be long gone, McHugh." The kitchen wasn't big enough for both of them, she thought. Dutton was overwhelming the space—and her—by doing nothing more than standing there in all his half-naked, masculine glory. At least she knew that the funny flutter in the pit of her stomach was caused by her shaky morning-after condition and had nothing to do with Dutton's presence. "Well?"

"Hey, relax," he said, rising both hands in a gesture of peace. "I made a pot of coffee, thinking we both could use some. Besides . . ." He ran one hand over his beard-roughened chin. "I need to spruce up a bit before I check into my hotel. I look like a bum. I came here straight from the airport, and my luggage is in your living room. You wouldn't mind if I took a quick shower and shaved, would you?"

"I . . .'"

"I did make the coffee. Even trade, don't you think?" He inched around her. "I'll be back in a flash." He beat a hasty retreat out of the kitchen.

"But ..." Bliss started. "Well, for Pete's sake." She stared at the coffee maker, momentarily mesmerized by the steady dripping of the fragrant liquid. "Well, one cup of coffee, *then* he's gone. One cup," she muttered, and pressed her hand to her forehead.

Dutton shaved, then stepped into the shower and let hot water beat against him. Heaven, he decided, and just what the doctor ordered to revive his poor body. Not only that, but being in the soothing shower meant he *wasn't* outside and headed for the hotel. He was still in the company of the enchanting Bliss Barton.

He'd heard about Steve's "pesty little sister" for years and had always been aware that despite Steve's brotherly complaints, he was extremely fond of Bliss. Dutton had sensed the loving bond between brother and sister and had known that if Bliss were ever in trouble, Steve would drop everything and rush to her aid. Steve had spoken often of his parents, too, with the same loving pride ringing in his voice.

Dutton frowned as he lathered with soap. They were a family, the Bartons, a real, close-knit family. He'd never grown tired of hearing about the Barton clan—the holiday traditions they'd shared over the years, the support and love they'd given each other.

Whenever a painful knot of envy had twisted within Dutton, he'd shoved it away and forced himself to make no comparisons between his own life and Steve's. There was no point in it. Facts were facts.

What he hadn't been prepared for, Dutton realized, was that Bliss was all grown up. She was a lovely woman, one who was causing a very grown up male reaction in him. Somehow, Steve's tales of his family during his visits had left the impression in Dutton's mind that his sister was a young, naive girl still on the brink of womanhood.

Dutton turned off the water and stepped onto a fluffy bath mat. As he absently began to dry himself, he searched his mind for things Steve had said about his sister.

He could not recall Steve's ever mentioning that Bliss was involved with a man. He had, in fact, spoken as though Bliss were much too young for a serious relationship. What else had Steve said? Something about . . . Yes, it was coming to him now. Steve had implied on more than one occasion that Bliss did not possess the "go for it" attitude of the Barton family. She was their conservative member, who walked a straight line, liked order and stability in her life.

Dutton smiled. No wonder she had screamed bloody murder when she'd found him next to her in bed. She was not accustomed, he was sure, to out-of-the-ordinary things happening in her well-ordered life.

His smile slowly changed to a frown as he dressed

in jeans and a gray sweater. Was he putting this together right, he wondered. Did Steve still envision Bliss as a young, innocent girl because she didn't possess the devil-may-care and go-with-the-flow attitudes of the Bartons? Didn't Steve realize that Bliss was a grown woman with a personality and code of conduct that was uniquely her own, albeit different from Steve's and the senior Barton's?

And what of Bliss? Dutton mused as he combed his damp hair. She'd said Steve had settled down a bit since falling in love with Mandy, and that she had heard of Steve and Dutton's "rowdy escapades." Stories, Dutton recalled, that Steve had said his folks would enjoy from start to finish. Bliss, apparently, didn't enjoy them.

Was it difficult for her, he wondered, to be smack-dab in the middle of a family she didn't fit in with? They all loved her, he was positive of that. But did she feel apart from them somehow—there, but not quite there? Was Bliss Barton lonely?

Dutton shook his head and left the steamy bathroom. McHugh, he told himself, can it. It wasn't like him to play amateur shrink, trying to figure out the complicated psyches of people around him. That Bliss Barton was taking up so much of his brain space was no doubt due to the throbbing he still felt in his head. After some coffee and a couple of aspirin, he'd be minding his own business, as he usually did. He'd see Bliss as the lovely-but-not-his-type younger sister of his best friend. End of story. Fine. That was exactly the way it should be.

With a decisive nod that he instantly regretted as pain shot through his head, Dutton left the bedroom, not bothering to put on his socks and shoes. As he passed through the living room again, he realized for the first time that the place was a mess from the night before. Glasses were here, there, and everywhere; ashtrays were overflowing; there were partially filled bowls of chips, pretzels, and dips. The carpet was strewn with empty champagne bottles, and chips and crackers that had been crushed by dancing feet.

Dutton stopped and glanced around. Beneath the clutter was a very nice apartment. The living room was quite large, and Bliss had decorated it in warm colors of brown, orange, and yellow. And it had a fireplace. Oh, yes, he did enjoy a roaring fire on a snowy night. Put on some soft music, sip brandy in the light of the glowing flames, then reach for Bliss and cover those sensuous lips of hers with his own.

He frowned. Reach for whom? Dammit, hadn't he just conducted a lengthy conversation with himself, and thoroughly agreed with himself, that Bliss was not his type, not on his agenda during his stay in Denver? Yes, he had.

She was his best friend's little sister, for cripes sake, forbidden territory. Besides that, he knew when a woman understood the rules of "no commitments, no promises, live for the moment." There were plenty of women like that in every city and country he'd ever been in, and Bliss Barton was definitely not one of them

Got it this time, McHugh? he asked himself dryly. A hangover and lack of healing coffee sure wreaked havoc with a man's thinking processes.

He left the living room and turned toward the kitchen, only to stop again. Bliss was sitting at the table in the small dining area adjacent to the kitchen. A mug of coffee was in front of her, and her elbows were resting on the table, her forehead nestled in her hands. Her auburn curls fell around her face and shoulders like a silken curtain.

She looked so small and fragile, he thought. He wanted to scoop her up and hold her close, tell her that she'd feel better, that her head would stop hurting, that nothing would hurt her because he was there now.

What? he asked himself. Where in the hell had that macho malarkey come from? He was no one's knight in shining armor, rushing to the rescue, slaying dragons in his path. He'd never intentionally run roughshod over anyone's feelings, but he certainly didn't have protective instincts either. He lived his life alone. Always had, always would. The only exception was Steve Barton, the one man he'd allowed close enough to call friend.

Dammit, he fumed, averting his eyes from Bliss and going into the kitchen. Bliss was throwing him totally out of kilter. No, no, it wasn't her, it was his headache.

He poured himself a mug of coffee, shook two aspirin into his hand from the bottle now sitting next to the coffee maker, and walked back into the dining area to sit across from her. He sipped the coffee, savoring its flavor, then swallowed the pills.

Bliss slowly lifted her head and looked at him.

Oh, damn, Dutton thought, it *was* Bliss who was throwing him for a loop. There was no way he could chalk up the sudden hot tightening in his lower body to a hangover. Those big blue eyes of hers were turning him inside out. And those lips . . . Lord, he wanted to taste those luscious lips, slip his tongue between them to meet hers, press her slender body against him. He wanted . . . yes, he wanted Bliss Barton.

He cleared his throat and took another deep swallow of coffee. "Feeling better?" he asked finally, staring into his mug.

Bliss nodded. "Some." Except for the funny flutter in the pit of her stomach, she added silently. Dutton McHugh was even better looking than she'd thought. Clean shaven, with his hair still damp, his pearl gray sweater accentuating his tan, he was incredible.

How could a man with such rugged, masculine features have lips that looked so soft? What would it be like to have those lips claim hers, kiss her until she couldn't think or breathe? What would it be like to have those powerful arms wrap around her, holding her close, pressing her to him? What would it be like to . . . Oh, mercy.

"Are *you* feeling better?" she asked.

He looked intently at her. "Some."

Neither moved. Their gazes held in a strange loss of time. Awareness and senses sharpened to a razor edge, and heartbeats echoed in their ears. A palpable tension crackled between them, spinning around them.

Bliss's breasts ached with a foreign heaviness.

Dutton's blood pounded through his veins.

Heat and pulsing desire swept through them, gathering force, and their heartbeats quickened.

"Bliss," Dutton said, his voice rough.

She blinked, then stiffened in her chair, her eyes widening. "I think . . . Yes, I need some more coffee." She stood and on trembling legs started toward the kitchen.

Dutton was instantly on his feet. He met her at the side of the table and lightly gripped her shoulders.

"Bliss . . ."

"Do you want more coffee?" she asked, her voice unsteady as she stared at his chest.

"In a minute. Bliss, something is happening here, between us. Don't you feel it?"

"No."

"Yes, you do. Look at me."

"No."

"Bliss, look at me."

She slowly raised her eyes to meet his.

"Yes, you do," he said, lowering his head toward

hers. "You feel it, just as I do. Don't you? Don't you, Bliss?"

"No, I . . . Yes . . ."

Do not kiss this woman! Dutton told himself.

She mustn't kiss this man! Bliss thought frantically.

He kissed her. Her lashes drifted down as his lips claimed hers, parted hers.

She raised her arms to encircle his neck. He dropped his hands from her shoulders to her back and pulled her to him, her breasts pressing against his muscled chest. The kiss deepened as they savored the taste of each other, along with the heated sensations rushing through them.

She had never been kissed like this, Bliss thought dreamily. Never before had she been filled with such instant overwhelming desire. Heat was throbbing deep within her, and her breasts ached with a sweet pain and that strange heaviness. She didn't want this kiss to end, not ever. Dutton McHugh was transporting her up and away from reality. Away . . . away . . .

Dutton's hands roamed over her back, then down to her buttocks to nestle her even closer to his aching body. She was surrendering to him, he thought exultantly, and his desire for her burned within him like nothing he'd experienced before. He could feel his control slipping out of his grasp, pulling him closer to the edge of no return.

He wanted Bliss Barton. And he would have her, now. She was telling him by the abandonment of her kiss, by the way she was molded against him, that her desire was as great as his. Nothing mattered but the two of them and what they would share. They would be sensational together, special, a joining more beautiful than any he had known. He and Bliss Barton . . . Barton . . . Steve Barton . . . Oh hell.

Dutton jerked his head up and drew a rough breath. He eased Bliss's arms from around his neck and caught her hands in his. She gazed up at him with eyes that were cloudy with desire.

"Bliss, we . . ." He paused, startled by the raspiness in his voice. "We have to stop. I know you want me as much as I want you, but . . ."

"What?" she whispered, then shook her head, as though clearing cobwebs from her mind. "Oh, good heavens, what am I doing? What are you doing?"

"*We* were doing it," he said, "and extremely well, I might add. You, Miss Barton, are not an innocent young girl, as Steve led me to believe."

She pulled her hands free and took a step backward. "I most certainly am. I mean, no, I'm not . . . a young girl, that is. Steve talks about me as though I were a child. I'm twenty-five years old, Mr. McHugh."

"Which Steve failed to mention. I thought his little sister was seventeen or eighteen. That kiss and the message that went with it were most definitely delivered by a woman.'"

"Message?"

"Like I said, you want me. Believe me, I want you,

too. Lord, do I want you. Your being Steve's sister got in my way, but that's my problem, and I'll deal with it." He reached for her. "Come here."

She smacked his hand and backed up even more, finally thudding against the wall. "I never said that I wanted you."

He advanced slowly toward her. "Didn't you?" His voice was low and rumbly, his eyes riveted on hers. "We burned together, Bliss, like a match being set to dry timber. Instantly hot and out of control, like a flash fire."

"No."

"Yes. Nothing like that has ever happened to me before." He stopped in front of her, his body inches from hers, and flattened his hands on the wall on either side of her head. "You felt it, I know you did. This is special, different. Right? Right, Bliss?"

Oh, yes, she thought, yes, yes, yes. "No. A kiss is a kiss." And she wanted him to kiss her again. "You're making far too much out of this." Kiss her for an hour, a day, a week, forever. "In fact, that kiss never should have taken place."

He flicked his tongue over her bottom lip. "Why not?" She shivered. "It was fantastic." His tongue outlined her upper lip. "Why shouldn't I kiss you again, and again?"

Darned if she knew why not, Bliss thought. It sounded like a wonderful idea. "Because . . . um . . ." *Think, Bliss!* "Oh! Yes, of course, I know why not. Because you're Dutton McHugh."

"You don't like my name?" His hands inched over to tangle in her wild curls. "I'll change it. What name do you want me to have?"

She pressed her hands flat on his chest and pushed, then gave up when she realized Dutton wasn't going to budge.

"Your name is fine," she said. "That's not the point. It's *who* you are."

"Who am I?"

"Steve's best friend, who has the same attitudes and outlooks as he does, or did before he met Mandy. The other half of the rowdy escapades, Steve's 'go-for-it buddy' of long standing. In short, Mr. McHugh, you and I have nothing in common." Except having shared an incredible kiss. "I don't think or operate on the same plane as my brother, or my parents for that matter. I'm a Barton, but not really. So, you see, since you're a carbon copy of Steve, you and I simply don't mix, mesh, whatever. Therefore, that kiss was a mistake, and it won't happen again." What a totally depressing thought

"That's a depressing thought." He brushed his lips over hers and felt her tremble. He'd figured Bliss out, right on the money, he realized. He was being lumped in with the Bartons, and she saw herself on the outside looking in. "You're not being fair. Just because I'm Steve's best friend doesn't mean I'm—"

A knock sounded at the door.

"The door," Bliss said brightly. "Fancy that. Well, well, I must go answer it. Excuse me?"

"Damn," Dutton said, backing away from her.

Bliss scooted around him and nearly ran to the door, flinging it open. "Mother!"

Jenny Barton came into the room. She was a tall, slender, and extremely attractive woman, with gray hair. She was dressed in a fuchsia sweat suit and running shoes.

"Hello, darling," she said, smiling at Bliss. "I was out for my run and decided to see how the party went last night. Your father is still fuming because I said you young people didn't need old fuddy-duddies at your wild bash. From the looks of this room, it was a huge success. I—" Her sweeping perusal fell on Dutton. "Well, now, this is interesting. Hello, young man. I'm Jenny Barton."

"Dutton McHugh,'" he said, walking into the living room.

"Oh, how wonderful," Jenny said, beaming. "We've been waiting years to meet you, Dutton. Welcome to Denver." She looked at Dutton's bare feet, then the fuzzy green and red slippers that Bliss wore. "This is getting more interesting by the moment."

"Mother," Bliss said, "this isn't what you think."

"Dutton didn't spend the night here?" Jenny asked.

"Well, yes, he did, but . . . Dutton, tell her."

"I spent the night here, Mrs. Barton," Dutton said pleasantly.

Jenny framed Bliss's face in her hands. "My darling child, you've chosen well. I feel as though I know

Dutton as I do my own son. You're a Barton after all, my sweetness. I'm thrilled for you both."

"But—" Bliss began.

"I must dash and finish my run," Jenny said. "Besides, I'm obviously interrupting. Have a marvelous day, dear. Good-bye for now, Dutton. I'm delighted that you're here. Absolutely delighted." She hurried out the door, closing it behind her.

Bliss slowly turned to face Dutton, fists planted on her hips, eyes narrowed.

Uh-oh, he thought.

"Dutton McHugh," she said through clenched teeth, "I'm going to strangle you with my bare hands!"

Two

"Hey, now, whoa, wait," Dutton said, raising his hands. "Stay calm, okay?"

"Calm?" Bliss said, nearly shrieking. "I have no intention of staying calm. I've been calm all of my life. I'm sick to death of being calm. Therefore, I refuse—are you getting this?—refuse to stay calm."

"The whole city is getting it," he said, grinning at her. "You've got great lungs, and a real temper to go with that dark red hair of yours."

Oh, yes, Dutton thought, there was a lot of passion in this delectable bundle. The kiss they'd shared had been only the tip of the iceberg. He'd felt the desire simmering in Bliss then. And now, passionately angry, she was magnificent. Her blue eyes were flashing, her cheeks were flushed, and she was breathing hard, causing her breasts to rise and fall enticingly. Dynamite.

"Look," he said, "it's not as though your mother is going to send your father and brother over here to beat me to a pulp. You're the only one upset, Bliss. Your mom was cool as a cucumber."

"Of course she was, you nincompoop. She thinks that I've finally broken free of my safe little cocoon and—and done it."

Dutton leaned toward her. "It?"

She waved her hands wildly in the air. "The big 'it.' Is my mother thrilled? You betcha, bub, because the man I chose to do 'it' with is a Barton clone. I can now receive the Barton stamp of approval on my forehead. I'll no longer make them nervous, edgy, wondering what to do with me or say to me. I've passed the test at long last by spending the night with the ever-famous Dutton McHugh, who is enough like Steve in thinking, values, and attitudes to qualify you two to be the Bobbsey Twins. And you stood there confirming my mother's beliefs by announcing that, 'Yes, indeedy-do, I spent the night with your darling Bliss.' I really would murder you, McHugh, but you're not worth going to jail for."

Dutton frowned and ran his hand over the back of his neck. "Hold it a minute here. It's hard to catch everything when you're screaming like a banshee." She made a noise that sounded suspiciously like a snort of disgust. "Are you saying that you're a—a virgin? No, forget that. There's no such thing as a twenty-five-year-old virgin." He paused. "Is there? Are you? Oh, holy hell, your mother thinks you've done . . . it . . . for the first time? With me? She said, 'You've chosen well.' What exactly does that mean?"

Bliss folded her arms over her breasts and smiled sweetly at him. "Why, Dutton dear, isn't it clear? For old-fashioned me to have taken this momentous step means that I have finally lost my heart, fallen in love, committed myself to the man of my dreams for all time. And to top it off, I've picked a man the family adores."

Dutton pressed one hand to his chest. "Me?"

"Who else? You told my mother yourself that you spent the night here."

"Well, yeah, but your parents are very open-minded. I know that Steve and Mandy have been living together for nearly a year, and your folks never blinked an eye. Steve and Mandy just decided last week to get married at Christmas and made the big announcement. Why would your mother jump to such extreme conclusions like love, commitment, the forever and ever jazz simply because you spent the night with a man?"

"Because I'm me. I'm conservative, cautious, and I think in a totally different way than my family does. I'm not saying they advocate casual sex, bed bouncing from here to the moon, but they've been very concerned because I'm twenty-five years old and haven't found anyone I cared enough about to . . . to . . ."

"Do 'it' with. I get the drift."

"My parents really do approve of Steve and Mandy's living together. Both my mother and my father come from broken homes, and their fervent hope is that neither of their children, or any future grandchildren, experience the heartbreak of divorce. Steve sowed his wild oats, much to my father's reminiscent delight, then he settled in with Mandy. Me? I haven't sowed anything, and I'm so far behind their schedule, they've been standing around wringing their hands, wondering what kind of genetic throwback I am."

"Until now," Dutton said glumly. "You've taken the big step, jumped right in, and done 'it.' "

"With the man I love." She batted her eyelashes at him. "Isn't that just the most romantic thing you ever did hear tell of? Good Lord, you must have a reputation as a fast worker. My mother knows I only met you last night at the party. Your track record must be a beaut."

"There's no reason to be rude, Bliss."

"I'm simply calling it as I see it," she said, shrugging. "Dutton McHugh comes, he scopes the territory, and he conquers. And this time? Mercy me, he's conquered the recalcitrant Miss Bliss Barton. A head-over-heels in love Bliss Barton, you understand, because otherwise I never would have done—"

"Don't say that dumb word again." He dragged a restless hand through his hair. "Now what happens?"

"Beats me. I've never been in this situation before. My mother has jogged home to share the exciting news with my father, I'm sure, and she's no doubt phoned Steve and Mandy."

"Wonderful," Dutton muttered.

"I can hear them now. Little Bliss is in love. Isn't that grand? And she's picked Dutton McHugh, a Barton if there ever was one. Isn't that super? She's a late bloomer, our Bliss, but she's gone for the gusto, made up for lost time, and—"

"Cut," he said, slicing a hand through the air. "Look, why can't we just sit them down and explain that nothing happened, that we sort of passed out and landed on the same bed?"

"They won't buy that for a second. They'll think I'm experiencing a rush of guilt, pat me on the head, and tell me I mustn't revert to my fuddy-duddy ways."

"What about me?"

"Well, my goodness, Dutton, they know I would never have allowed you to spend the night if you hadn't declared your love for me. And, of course, your honorable intentions."

His dark eyebrows shot up. "My what?"

"You intend to marry me."

"What!"

"Oh, yes. I shouldn't have said you have a reputation as a fast worker. After all, you fell in love with me at first sight, just as I did with you. You look a bit pale, Dutton. Is your headache worse?"

"Bliss, we're in a heap of trouble here. Your family thinks that we . . . we . . ."

"Did 'it,' " she said decisively.

"Would you quit saying that? I really hate the way that sounds."

"Well, excuse me, Mr. McHugh."

"And now they believe we're going to be married?"

"Yep, that's how I figure it. Well, I guess I'd better start cleaning up this place. Steve and Mandy sure have messy friends. I agreed to have the party here because they're in the middle of renovating that big old house they bought. I didn't know the majority of the people who were here last night."

"And now you're supposedly going to marry one of them." He shook his head. "This is unbelievable, really insane. Bliss, has it ever occurred to you that your family is a little nuts? I realize that Steve is my best friend, but . . . He knows I'm not the marrying kind. No, that won't wash. He used to say that about himself. This is a hell of a mess. How can you be so calm?"

"I pride myself on staying calm during stressful situations. I know I lost it for a bit earlier, but I'm under control again. That doesn't mean I have a solution to this fiasco. I simply refuse to get hysterical about it."

"What are we going to say when we see your family?"

"I don't have the foggiest notion." She began to collect glasses from an end table.

Dutton frowned as he watched Bliss pick up as many glasses as she could carry and take them into the kitchen. A moment later he heard noises indicating that she was loading the dishwasher. He absently began to stack the bowls containing the remnants of chips, crackers, and pretzels.

Interesting, he mused. One minute Bliss was all spit and fire, letting loose with unbridled passionate anger that had made him want to haul her into his arms and kiss her senseless. Now it was as though she'd pulled a plug on her emotions, slid behind an invisible shield that she labeled her usual calm composure, and was going about her business as if nothing out of the ordinary had happened.

And that, Dutton surmised, stacking his tower of bowls higher, was how Bliss survived being a Barton who walked to the beat of a different drummer. She hid, within herself. Behind her wall of calmness, she shut out the chaotic world and off-beat personalities of the other Bartons, not allowing her space to be invaded.

But not this time, he vowed, starting toward the kitchen. This scenario that she was retreating from included him. They were in this together, by damn. *He* was the man who had spent the night with her. *He* was the man that the Bartons assumed was the love of her life. *He* was the man supposedly planning to marry Bliss Barton.

Dutton stopped abruptly, the bowls teetering precariously. He and she were in this together, he repeated. Together. Bliss and Dutton. Dutton and Bliss. Together was a word he'd never associated with himself and anyone else. He was a loner—first because of circumstances beyond his control, then by choice. He'd gotten along just fine alone for the majority of his thirty-two years, and he intended to live out his days in the same manner. He'd allowed only Steve Barton to step inside the invisible circle he drew around himself, and Dutton had never regretted that.

Oh, yes, he thought, he understood the wall Bliss retreated behind, as his circle served the same purpose. It was safe there. What couldn't be touched, couldn't be hurt. But there would be no walls, no circles, this time, because he and Bliss were in this together. And for some unexplainable reason, he liked the way that sounded.

Bliss zipped out of the kitchen, glanced at Dutton and his tower of bowls, then continued past him to collect more glasses. As Dutton disappeared into the kitchen she picked up two more glasses, then stopped, a glass in each hand.

Oh, Lord, she thought, she was in the midst of a living nightmare. Like dominoes falling one into the next, the horrifying events had taken place so quickly, there had been no chance of stopping them.

Waking up with a strange man hadn't been enough, she thought dismally. She'd had to kiss said man with a passion she'd never dreamed she was capable of. The next domino, the scene with her mother, was almost more than she could bear thinking about. All the Bartons no doubt had heard by now that she had spent the night with Dutton McHugh, was in love with Dutton McHugh, and was going to marry Dutton McHugh.

And to top it off, she'd actually stood there explaining to Dutton that she was a virgin. That personal condition was one she wasn't thrilled about, but she had accepted it as the way it was and the way it was likely to remain. She certainly didn't go around having an in-depth conversation on the subject with anyone, especially a man she hardly knew.

What on earth was she going to do about this entire disaster? she wondered. She'd managed to plaster her calm, plastic smile on her face, presenting to Dutton a picture of someone in control and placing little importance on the situation at hand.

But she wasn't calm!

She was on the verge of hysteria!

She was all alone against the rest of the Bartons, and she didn't know what to do, or say, or—

"You're not alone, you know."

She gasped and spun around, holding the two glasses tightly to her chest. She met Dutton's dark gaze and felt, once again, the funny flutter in her stomach.

"Pardon me?" she said, a breathless quality to her voice. Oh, he was so gorgeous, so magnificently masculine, so strong and virile. His kiss, the feel of his muscled body, his taste and aroma, had been ecstasy.

He took the glasses from her and set them on the

end table. Circling her slender neck with his hands, he gently stroked her soft cheeks with his thumbs.

"I said that you're not alone," he repeated, his voice low. "We're in this thing together, Bliss. Understand?"

Together, Bliss thought. What a lovely word, and one that had never really applied to her. She was alone, not by choice, but because that was just how it was. Together with Dutton? The idea gave her a warm feeling inside, as if a comforting blanket were being tucked around her with special care. But, no, it wasn't true. She wasn't "together" with Dutton McHugh.

"No, Dutton," she said, "this really isn't your problem. It's not your fault that my family is a tad eccentric, or whatever you want to call them. You came to Denver to be Steve's best man at the wedding in two weeks. You certainly didn't ask for this mess we're . . . I'm in. I'll deal with my family. When they ask you about this, just say they should speak to me."

"And what will you say to them?" he asked. He continued to stroke her cheeks with a steady rhythm.

"I don't know yet, but I'll straighten all of this out . . . somehow." How was it possible that the soft stroking of Dutton's thumbs could make her feel as though she were melting inside, just dissolving? Such heat was churning deep within her, an insistent heat that was pulsing to the rhythm of Dutton's thumbs. "Thank you for taking those bowls to the kitchen. I'll finish cleaning up here. I'm sure you're eager to get settled into your hotel. Well . . . um . . . good-bye, Dutton."

"No."

"No?"

"Bliss, I'm the one who crashed on your bed last night. If it weren't for me, your family wouldn't have any reason to believe that we . . . that you and I . . . Well, you know. Granted, your mother went a little nuts with the information. I mean, Lord, in today's society when two adults spend the night together, it doesn't automatically lead to a trip to the altar."

"My mother assumed it did because—"

"Yes, I know, because you are who you are, and I respect that. And I respect you, Bliss. I have no intention of leaving you alone to face the ramifications of this thing. So, I repeat, we're in this together. We'll get it squared away, you'll see."

"No, I—"

"Bliss, don't argue," he said, then covered her lips with his.

Argue because Dutton's lips were once again sending wonderous sensations swirling within her? she wondered. Argue about the fact that he tasted so good, and felt so good, and his tongue was rubbing against hers in a rhythm that matched the one of his thumbs on her cheeks and the pulsing heat deep inside her? Argue? She wouldn't dream of it.

Dutton slid his hands from Bliss's throat to her silken curls. As she wrapped her arms around his waist and pressed against him, his body reacted in instant, aching arousal. To touch Bliss, to kiss Bliss, to inhale the aroma of sweet, sweet Bliss, was to ignite a raging flame of desire within him, a flash fire bursting wildly out of control.

He had *never* wanted a woman as he did Bliss. And he had never felt protective toward a woman, wanting to tell her he would keep her safe from harm. Something new and strange was happening to him. He didn't know for certain if he liked this, and he was torn between an urge to run and a driving need to stay.

Together, his mind echoed. They were in this together. That sounded so damn good. Where would he run to? His swanky apartment in San Francisco, which was beautifully furnished but didn't have a warmth of welcome when he walked in the door?

He plunged his tongue deep into her mouth, dropping his arms to encircle her, pull her closer, nestling her hips against his.

Run? he asked himself hazily. To the beds of women whose faces were now a blur, their names forgotten? Run, just when he was vaguely realizing that he had, at long last, come home? Dear Lord, what was Bliss Barton doing to him?

He broke the kiss and buried his face in her fragrant hair, waiting for his breathing to quiet before he attempted to speak.

"Bliss," he said finally, gently moving her away from him, "enough. I can't handle any more right now."

"I . . ." She took a shaky breath. "I'm sorry. I shouldn't have kissed you again. You make me feel so . . . I've never felt such . . . But I'm not a tease, Dutton. It's just that when you kiss me I can't seem to think straight."

He took a step back, dragging one hand through his hair. "Tell me about it," he said gruffly. "My mind takes off down roads I didn't even know existed. I really don't know what's happening here, Bliss. One minute I want to discover exactly what this is between us, and in the next breath I want to get the hell out of here." He pushed his hands into his pockets and stared up at the ceiling, willing his body back under control. He met her gaze again. "I think I'd better check into my hotel."

"Yes, all right," she said quietly.

"Oh, damn, I *can't* leave. What if your family shows up? I told you we were in this together, and I meant it? You could end up facing the Barton inquisition alone. We have to decide how we're going to handle this, what to say. Don't they know there's no such thing as love at first sight and all that romantic malarkey?" Or was there, he wondered. "We only met last night, for Pete's sake."

"And I don't even remember meeting you," she said, shaking her head. "As for love at first sight, my parents got married twenty-six hours after they met."

"Terrific," he said dryly. "That's a typical Barton move. They're really going to buy this, aren't they?

We met last night, took one look at each other, and
. . . whamo . . . fell in love." He snapped his fingers.
"Just like that."

She sighed. "I'm afraid so. You want to know how
my parents met? They were stuck in an elevator
together for three hours. By the time they were
rescued, they knew they were in love. They flew to
Las Vegas the next day and were married. Twenty-
six hours after being caught between the eighth and
ninth floors."

"That doesn't make sense, Bliss. You said they
were all in favor of Steve and Mandy's living together
and being very sure of their relationship before
committing themselves to marriage so they could try
to avoid the horrors of divorce. How do your folks
justify having dashed off to Vegas to be married only
a day after they met?"

"Dutton, Jenny and Sam Barton don't justify
anything they do. If it feels right to them and they're
in agreement, they do it. They don't seek anyone's
approval but each other's. Steve and Mandy are the
same way. If my folks had pitched a fit because they
were living together, Steve and Mandy wouldn't have
changed their minds. Steve grew up with that attitude
and, fortunately, found a woman who thinks the
way he does. It just happens that they decided to
buy that old house and fix it up. Believe me, if
they'd decided to live in a tent on a mountaintop,
they would have done it."

"Yeah, you're right. Steve has had that 'if it feels

right, do it' attitude as long as I've known him. He got himself, and me, into more than one tight spot because of it. I always went along with him because I figured, what the hell. I didn't have anyone to answer to except myself. I still don't."

"No one? What about your family?"

"No one," he repeated. "So, okay, I'm getting the picture now. Your parents didn't question Steve and Mandy's decision to live together, but they would also understand love at first sight, because that's what happened to them. If you try to deny that anything happened last night, they'll shrug that off as your having a case of the guilts. Have I got this right so far?"

"Yes, I'd say so."

He shoved his hands into his back pockets and began to pace the floor. Bliss watched him trek back and forth for several minutes.

"Dutton," she said finally, "you're going to wear out my carpet."

"Shh. I'm thinking."

She rolled her eyes, crossed her arms over her breasts, and tapped one foot. Dutton continued to pace.

No one, she thought suddenly. Dutton had no family, no one? How many years had he been alone? While there were endless times when she felt separated from her family, she always knew they were there for her.

She stopped the impatient tapping of her foot and frowned as she studied Dutton.

He had no one. Oh, she was very certain he had women whenever the mood struck, but casual affairs didn't come close to providing the warmth, support, and love that a family did. Dutton was alone, and apparently he preferred it that way, for he'd surely had the opportunity to marry.

Goodness, she thought, Dutton must feel like a trapped animal because of this ridiculous situation they were in. He was a free spirit, who was suddenly caught up in a phony scenario of having fallen in love and committed himself to her for all time. His statement that they were in this together had sounded lovely, but he didn't mean it, not really. He was a loner. Any second now he'd stop his trek across her living room and tell her he couldn't handle this after all. He'd cut and run, and she'd understand why he had to. Yet with that understanding, she already knew, would come a lingering and unexplainable sadness and sense of loss.

Dutton halted his pacing so suddenly that she jumped in surprise.

"I have a plan," he said, pulling his hands out of his pockets.

This was it, she thought. This was where he announced he was returning to San Francisco for whatever reason. He'd have some story concocted for Steve as to why he couldn't attend the wedding, then, poof, Dutton would be gone. She'd never see him again. Never share another of those incredible kisses. Never feel the new and wonderous desire churning within her. The ache in her throat warned her she was amazingly close to bursting into tears.

"Bliss, are you with me?"

"What? Oh, yes, go ahead. I'm listening."

"Okay, here it is."

Good-bye, Dutton McHugh. Oh, she was hating this.

"Your folks have covered all the bases. They believe in love at first sight, yet also go with living together to be certain all is well. Those are polar opposite viewpoints, but Bartons are Bartons so . . . Anyway, they'll never buy that nothing happened between us, so we'll have to play this out."

"What?" she said. Where was cut and run? Going back to San Francisco? Where was the good-bye?

"Bliss, are you paying attention?"

"Yes, of course."

"Instead of picking one way to go, we'll combine the two."

"Huh?"

"Look, they believe we're in love. So, we give them love at first sight."

"We do?"

"Yep." Dutton was beginning to appear extremely pleased with himself. "But then we switch to the other channel. Instead of dashing off to Vegas to get married, we decide, even though we're madly in love, to live together first. That will fit in nicely with your basically cautious nature. Marriage is, after all, a very big step."

"What are you saying?" she whispered.

"Then, gosh and golly, we discover we're totally incompatible. We'll wait until after Steve and Mandy get married to announce that, so we don't put a damper on things for them. Your folks will be distressed that we didn't make it together, but once they think it through, they'll be grateful that their Bliss didn't suffer the horrors of divorce."

"Hold it, McHugh. Are you suggesting—"

"I knew you weren't completely paying attention, Bliss. What I just clearly explained here is the most reasonable and, I must say, most brilliant solution to this dilemma."

She leaned toward him. "Spell it out for me in very small words."

"Certainly. Sweet Bliss Barton, I, Dutton McHugh, am, as of this moment, this point in time—"

"Dutton!"

He grinned. "—living with you."

Three

A cold front moved into Denver in the late morning, pushing aside the unseasonably warm weather that had allowed Jenny Barton to take her run clad only in a fleece-lined jogging suit. With the drop in temperature came huge, wet flakes of snow that began to transform the city into a glittering fairyland. A chill wind accompanied the snow and seemed to carry with it the spirit of Christmas, to match the bright decorations on the streetlight poles and the holiday displays in the store windows.

People who were out and about were smiling, walking with a spring in their step as the contagious feeling of Christmas cheer spread. Children's laughter danced through the air, and the Santa Clauses on the corners rang their bells with vigor. Christmas was a little more than two weeks away, and Denver, Colorado, was eager and excited.

Dutton walked slowly along the sidewalk, staying close to the buildings to keep out of the bustling pedestrian traffic. His hands shoved into the pockets of his sheepskin jacket, he barely noticed the snow floating over him, dotting his dark hair. He glanced unseeing into the lavishly decorated store windows.

He was attempting—and failing miserably—to determine exactly how he felt about the bizarre events that had taken place that morning. While he assumed he knew himself as well as any person who kept in touch with his inner self, he was admittedly confused by the roller coaster rise and fall of his emotions. He was, in short, a befuddled mess.

Enough of this, he told himself firmly. Bliss Barton was the source of his mental upheaval, that much was certain. Bliss Barton, with her curly auburn hair and sparkling blue eyes, was turning him inside out. Desire still smoldered within him like embers not fully extinguished, embers that could burst into a raging fire at the slightest provocation.

Lord, he wanted her, wanted to make love to her in front of the fireplace in the glow of burning logs. He would remove her clothes slowly, kissing every inch of her skin as it was revealed. He would be gentle with her, careful, controlling his rampant passion as he showed her the magic of making love. He'd do nothing to hurt or frighten her as he claimed her as his.

Dutton glanced quickly at the passing people, having the irrational thought that everyone could read his mind, see the erotic scenario he was creating, feel the heat pulsing through him. No one, he realized to his relief, was paying the least bit of attention to him.

So far, he thought dryly, he was accomplishing nothing toward sorting through the jumble in his mind. That he wanted Bliss was a given, and envisioning her naked and responsive in his arms was tying him in knots. He had to forget his body and concentrate on his brain.

When he had told Bliss of his plan to move in with her, she had stared at him with her mouth open and her eyes as big as saucers. Without giving her a chance to respond to what he'd said, he'd grabbed his shoes, socks, and jacket, and told her to think it over. He'd get out of her way for now, he'd blithered on, so she'd have an opportunity to sort it through and realize it was a great solution to their wacko problem.

Then he'd hightailed it out the door, panicked at the thought that he'd hear Bliss yelling after him not to darken her doorway again. To his relief, she remained in shocked silence, and he'd hit the street to find that snow had arrived in Denver.

Now, there he was an hour later, trudging along

with wet, cold feet, wondering why on earth he'd been so determined to take up residence at Bliss's. He could simply tell the Bartons to knock off their nonsense, then check into his hotel, and that would be that. But, oh, no, not Dutton McHugh. He was ready to move heaven and earth to convince Bliss that his plan was the only workable solution.

Why?

So that he could seduce Bliss, make love to her?

Hey, she wanted him, too, he rationalized. That had been apparent when he'd pulled her into his arms and kissed her.

But she was a virgin.

If he became Bliss's first lover, he would be taking on a tremendous responsibility, not only for her delicate body, but for the emotional impact on her.

"Lord," Dutton said, running one hand down his face. He stopped in front of a store and stared blindly at the brightly colored toys in the window.

He wasn't accomplishing a thing, he decided, except becoming very adept at chasing his own thoughts around his brain in a never-ending circle. He was also freezing to death. He had never been so confused, and he didn't like it, not one damn bit.

He spun around and headed back in the direction he'd come, remembering that he'd seen a small café a ways back. Not only was he freezing, he was also hungry, really starving. Maybe food would increase his brain power, make the answers he needed light up like neon signs.

"Somehow," he muttered, "I doubt it."

Bliss cleaned the apartment until there was no trace of the boisterous, fun-loving crowd that had been there the night before.

What she could not erase, she knew, was the last lingering throbbing of her headache. It obviously had moved in for the day. Also stamped indelibly in her mind were the unbelievable-but-true events starring her and Dutton McHugh. The headache would disappear in hours; Dutton would not.

"Dutton the Domino," she said, with a weak little giggle. She sank onto the sofa and massaged her aching temples with her fingertips. She'd opened her eyes that morning to find Dutton beside her in the bed, and the dominoes had begun to fall immediately.

And the latest one was Dutton's statement that he should move into her apartment!

That was the last straw, Bliss decided. Enough was enough. She had no intention of going one step further in this charade in order to please her family. She would tell them it was all a mistake, that she was still the cautious, out-of-it Bliss she had always been, and they should go on as before, wringing their hands and clicking their tongues in dismay.

Oh, dear, she thought miserably, what a dreary picture that painted in her mind. At her age, she supposed it shouldn't be so important to be totally accepted by her family, yet it was, because she'd never achieved that goal. All of her life she'd struggled to be like them, but had always fallen short of the mark. At twenty-five years old, it shouldn't matter, but it did, it really did.

And now Dutton McHugh was there.

Dutton, who, for some reason, was willing to be her partner in crime, cohort in a diabolical plan that would gift wrap and present to Bliss the Barton clan's total acceptance of who she was.

All she had to do was live with Dutton McHugh.

"Oh," she moaned, "this is crazy."

Or was it?

Bliss tapped one fingertip against her chin. Two weeks, she mused. That was all it would take. And it would be a busy two weeks, because of the holiday season and Steve and Mandy's pending wedding. There wouldn't be an overabundance of spare time for family get-togethers, and when the Bartons did gather, she and Dutton would appear to be deliriously in love. Then after the wedding and Christmas, they'd announce that they just weren't suited for each other, and Dutton would ride off into the sunset to San Francisco. Perfect.

"Perfectly depressing," Bliss muttered. No, no, it was a good plan, a great plan. Her family would see her in a new light, as one of the group. They'd commiserate over her failed love affair, she'd assure them she would be fine, and life would go on with her new status there for her to enjoy. Yes, life would go on.

Without Dutton.

His smile, his kiss, the very essence of him had touched her deep within, awakened a passion and need she hadn't known she possessed. When he drew her into his arms, holding her tightly against his strong body, her cautious nature fled, and she only savored the new and wondrous sensations rushing through her.

And for two weeks, Dutton could be hers.

"Oh, now, you just hold it, Bliss Barton," she said aloud. She was getting carried away, swept up in the charade. She wasn't really a go-for-it gal, she was only going to pretend to be one. She had no intention of actually living with Dutton in every sense of the word. She wasn't going to do "it"!

And Dutton knew that. Didn't he?

She pressed her hands to her suddenly flushed cheeks. She'd been so stunned by Dutton's proposed plan that she'd simply stared at him like an idiot. Before she'd had a chance to see if her voice was working, he'd zoomed out the door. She'd never gotten the nitty-gritty details of his marvelous solution that they live together until after Steve and Mandy's wedding.

"Well, I've got news for you, McHugh," she said, getting to her feet. "There will be no hanky-panky in this establishment." Well, a few kisses here and there would be acceptable. Very nice, as a matter of fact. No, maybe that wasn't a good idea. But then again—

A knock at the door pulled her from her mental debate.

"Oh, goodness," she said, after opening the door, "Dutton, you're covered in snow."

He came into the room and unbuttoned his jacket. "It's really coming down out there."

"That's wonderful," she said, smiling. "I'm going to get my Christmas decorations out. I was waiting until after the party, and now there's even snow to set the mood. Just hang your jacket over the shower rod in the bathroom."

He nodded and headed for the bathroom. When he returned to the living room, Bliss was pulling boxes from the closet by the door.

"Bliss," he said, "did you think about what I said?"

She straightened and turned to look at him. "Yes. I got so excited about the snow and getting ready for Christmas that I forgot for a minute. I adore Christmas, don't you? I love the decorations, and shopping in the crowds. I even like the blaring, piped-in carols in the malls, and—"

"Bliss."

"I watch the kids sitting on Santa's lap and—"

"Bliss, hold it. You're talking a hundred miles an hour."

"I am? Well, I'm excited about Christmas and— When you say 'living together,' do you mean 'living together'? Or do you mean just sort of being together while we're living, but not really 'living together'?"

He blinked. "Could you run that by me a little slower?"

"Oh." She frowned. "What I'm trying to determine here is what you had in mind when you came up with your so-called brilliant plan. You failed to cover the details, you see."

A slow smile crept onto his face, a very male smile, as he crossed his arms loosely over his chest.

"Details," he said, nodding. "Well, yes, I can understand why you'd want the details. Will we share the cooking and cleaning up? Do I leave my dirty socks on the floor, or toothpaste in the sink? Yes, I guess we have some things to discuss. And, of course, there's the subject of . . ."

She leaned toward him. "Yes?"

His smile grew bigger. "Expenses. I don't intend to mooch. I'll pay my fair share."

"No, no, that isn't necessary. After all, Dutton, you're doing this because of my screwball family. Your plan will actually make them believe that I'm not a hopeless case, but a Barton through and through. I appreciate your willingness to help me. If you stay, you'll do so as my guest, but I'm sure the hotel where you have your reservation is much more comfortable than my apartment."

"You have a very nice apartment. Besides, Bliss, don't make me out to be too much of a hero." His smile faded. "We both know that no one in your family is going to believe that nothing happened here last night. If I insist on denying it and move to my hotel, I run the risk of losing Steve's friendship. Plus . . . well, I think I'll enjoy feeling that I belong in a family like yours, even for a couple of weeks. So, you see, we're in this together, and we both have a lot to gain."

"You really don't have any family? What happened to them?"

"Nothing fancy. My dad split when I was born, my mother died when I was four. I was raised in foster homes. End of story."

"But who do you usually spend Christmas with?"

He shrugged. "I don't pay much attention to the holidays. They come, they go. Look, I was just stringing you along a few minutes ago, giving you a hard time. Your family will buy the charade, think we're living together in every sense of the term, but I'll be sleeping on the sofa."

Well, darn, Bliss thought. Oh, for heaven's sake, shame on her. Where had that naughty, wanton reaction come from?

"When we're with a Barton, we'll play our parts," he went on. "I've never been in love, but it can't be that tough to act out. We gaze at each other and sigh a lot, I think. I don't know, we'll watch Steve and Mandy and pick up pointers. But when we're alone, we'll behave like—like buddies, pals." Not touch her? he thought. Not kiss her? Lord, he had to be out of his mind to agree to this. "Get it?"

He wasn't going to kiss her, or touch her, or hold her? Bliss wondered. What a rotten plan. "Got it."

"Then we're in agreement?"

"It's a deal, McHugh," she said, extending her hand.

He looked at her hand, her face, then her hand again. He took her small hand in his, but held it rather than give it a brisk shake, held it firmly in his own as their eyes met again.

Such strength and heat in that hand, Bliss thought. The warmth was traveling up her arm, tingling across her breasts, and sizzling down to that dark, pulsing place within her.

She stared into his eyes, thinking that she couldn't remember ever seeing eyes that were as dark as his. What sadness must have shown in those eyes when he was a lonely little boy with no family to call his own. Even now he had no one. Christmas came and went for him with none of the joy, the excitement, the secret presents.

Well, not this year, she decided. He was going to be there with her, share in the festivities, be a part of a family. He'd experience all the wonder that went with the holiday. They'd decorate the apartment, buy a tree and trim it, go shopping in the crowds that buzzed with excitement and Christmas cheer. Oh, yes, this was going to be a fantastic time for them, for her and Dutton, together.

"When do we put this plan in motion?" she asked, hearing the thread of breathlessness in her voice.

He slipped his free hand to the nape of her neck. "Right after . . ." He dropped her hand as he stepped closer to her, then he wrapped his arm around her shoulders. ". . . I kiss you."

"Oh," she said, then no more, as his lips captured

hers. She didn't want this to be the last kiss they would share! She didn't want this to be the last time she would nestle close to his firm body, savoring his heat, inhaling his aroma, which was fresh air and soap and him. She didn't want to begin to play the role of Dutton's lover. Because she wanted it to be real.

The kiss had been soft and gentle at first, but quickly deepened to a searing, hungry, urgent mating of lips and tongues. Hands roamed over fleecy sweaters, seeking what was beneath. Their heartbeats quickened, and their breathing became labored, echoing in the quiet room.

Sweet, sweet Bliss, Dutton thought. Each time he took her into his arms she gave more, so openly, honestly. Damn, she was so trusting. He could seduce her, he knew that, because in her innocence she surrendered all to his kiss, holding nothing back. Yes, he could seduce her, make her his, ease the burning ache in his body. But he wouldn't, because this was Bliss. It was as simple and as confusing as that.

He raised his head, and she opened her eyes. Framing her face in his hands, he stroked her cheeks with his thumbs. Gazing at each other, their bodies still pressed close, neither wished to break the spell, to end the sensual, magical moment.

Then Bliss sighed, an unsteady, sad sigh, and took a step backward.

Dutton nodded, but didn't speak, as he shoved his hands into his back pockets.

Yet still their gazes held, reflecting their desire. The words that would reveal that passion remained unspoken, though. To say aloud what their bodies were aching for would mean risking that it would happen. This wasn't the time.

Bliss broke the silence that hung heavily in the air. "Well . . ." she said.

"Yeah," Dutton said gruffly. He tore his gaze from hers and glanced around the room. "You sure spruced up the place."

"It's as good as new," she said, managing a small smile. "No one would ever know there'd been a party here."

He looked at her again. "But there was, and I came."

"Yes, I know, Dutton," she whispered. "You came . . . for a while."

"And now I'm going to stay."

"For a while."

Wrong, he thought suddenly. He was going to stay for the rest of his life. He was going to pull Bliss back into his arms and never let her go. Oh, hell, that was nuts. He was getting carried away in the heat of the moment. Whatever this was that was happening between him and Bliss, it didn't include forever. To even contemplate such a thing meant that somewhere in the recesses of his mind he was wondering if he was falling in love with Bliss Barton. Well, forget that. He lived alone.

A sharp knock at the door caused both of them to

jerk in surprise. The knock came again before Bliss had a chance to open the door. When she did, Steve strode into the room, a stormy expression on his face. He was slightly shorter than Dutton and not as muscular, yet he was a handsome man. He had dark auburn hair the same shade as Bliss's, and the same blue eyes.

"Uh-oh," Dutton said, under his breath. "Now it begins."

Steve spun around to face them. "I heard about you two from Mom. I'm happy for you, I really am. That's how it goes, you know. One minute you're minding your own business, then . . . whamo . . . you're a goner. My sister and my best friend. It's great. I'm glad things went this way for you. I'd just about chalked both of you up as hopeless cases, but the old love bug got down to serious business."

"If you're so thrilled," Bliss said, "why do you look so crabby?"

"It's not because of you two and what's going on here. Damn it, it's Mandy. We had a wingdinger of an argument this morning." He flopped down on the sofa, then in the next instant was back on his feet, pacing the floor with heavy steps.

"Care to share?" Dutton asked, raising his eyebrows.

Steve stopped and threw his arms open wide. "Mandy wants to have a baby!"

"Oh, how sweet," Bliss said.

"It is not!" Steve yelled.

"Oh," she mumbled. "Sorry."

Dutton frowned. "Why isn't it sweet? I mean, what is your problem, Steve? Babies are cute . . . little people or . . ." he shrugged. "Whatever. Hell, I don't know. What are you so steamed up about?"

"Whenever Mandy and I have talked about our future, she's never said one word about a baby before. Not one. Barton Property Management is growing bigger all the time, our reputation is spreading, we've moved into Aspen, Vail, a lot of the skiing areas, renting out and maintaining people's vacation homes. We've tripled our listings in the last year."

"You sound like a radio commercial," Bliss said. "What has the success of the business got to do with—"

"I have more expansion plans," Steve went on. "Mandy and I were to travel farther for even more listings. We'd have the house we're fixing up as our home base, but we'd spend the majority of the time on the road. Mom and Dad would stay in the office here."

"Excuse me, Steve Barton," Bliss said, "but I work in that office too. Why didn't I know about these new ideas of yours? This affects me, you know. I do all the bookkeeping for those listings, send out the monthly statements, and—"

"I know, I know," Steve interrupted. "That's why I asked Dutton to come over two weeks before the wedding. I want him to analyze the setup at the office, with the goal of putting all your work on a computer program."

"What?" Bliss said, her eyes widening. "My work? I don't know anything about computers. I hate computers. They sit there staring at me like they're smarter than I am. I've developed my own bookkeeping system and it works just fine, thank you very much."

"You're just barely keeping up," Steve said, "and you're putting in longer and longer hours."

"So you brought Dutton here to computerize me? Why didn't you talk this over with me first?"

"You hate change, Bliss. You like the status quo, having things go on as they always have. I decided it was better to wait until Dutton was here to explain things to you, show you how much easier your job would be if all the records were on a computer. That's what Dutton does, you know. He goes into companies and figures out the best computer system for them."

"No, I didn't know," she said, crossing her arms over her breasts, "and I really resent this. You've all had a bunch of meetings that I knew nothing about."

"Bliss," Dutton said, "take it easy."

She shot him a dark glare. "I certainly will not."

"If you'd known ahead of time," Steve said, "you would have dug in your heels and refused to listen to one word Dutton said. This way, he's here, ready to show you what he's talking about. Mom and Dad want to go on computer, Bliss, and they knew you'd fight any upset in your routine. They were all in favor of Dutton's coming in early."

"Oh, man," Dutton said, shaking his head. "Your mouth is your worst enemy, Steve."

Bliss turned on him. "You knew all about this, didn't you, Dutton?"

"Yes. No. Bliss, Steve told me what he wanted me to do here, and that it involved your area of the family business, but you have to remember that I thought you were much younger than you are. I figured you were snowed under by work and—"

"Mr. McHugh, may I ask you why you failed to mention all this to me since you arrived?"

"Because," Steve said, "he's been busy falling in love with you and . . . stuff."

"Stuff?" Bliss yelled.

"Yeah," Steve said. "You know . . . stuff."

Dutton closed his eyes and shook his head again.

"Steve Barton, I'm going to—"

"Don't holler at me, Bliss," Steve said. "Mandy and I just went ten rounds, and I'm an emotionally depleted man." He slouched onto the sofa again, but this time stayed put.

"Your jacket is wet from the snow," Bliss said. "Get off my sofa."

Dutton chuckled as he walked over to Steve and extended his hand for the jacket. Steve shrugged out of the coat and gave it to Dutton, who took it into the bathroom. When Dutton returned, Bliss's arms were crossed over her chest. She was tapping one foot and scowling at a spot on the far wall. Steve was staring at a throw pillow on the sofa, looking totally miserable.

"Well . . . um . . ." Dutton started, then cleared his throat. "Look, there's two issues to be covered here. It seems to me"—he gave Bliss a hard look—"that first up should be Steve's distress about Mandy. Don't you agree, Bliss?"

Her features softened. "Yes. Yes, of course. Not that the other subject is going to be ignored, you understand, but . . . Steve, you and Mandy have been going together for over a year and a half. You never discussed children before?"

"No. I met her when she did that brochure for the business, remember? When she was working for that ad agency, before Dad hired her to do our advertising? Since then our focus has been on each other and how to make Barton Property Management grow. When we bought the house two months ago, she was so excited. She said she'd always wanted to fix up an old place like that. It was her idea to sell off the furniture from the apartment and rough it until the place was ready for new things. She's a real trouper and has worked every bit as hard as I have on that old place."

Dutton sat down in a straight chair. "Go on."

"Last night after we got home from the party, Mandy said it was really sinking in that we were going to be married. I mean, it was just a week ago that I told her we should quit messing around and make it legal, and she agreed."

Bliss started across the room toward him, scowling again. "That's how you proposed? You said, 'Let's quit messing around and make this legal'? That's as romantic as a wet dishrag! Honestly, Steve, you could have—Oh!" Dutton grabbed her around the waist and pulled her onto his lap. "What are you—"

He grinned at her. "Never let it be said that Dutton McHugh is as romantic as a wet dishrag. No, sir, not me. Carry on with your story, Steve."

Bliss attempted to slide off Dutton's lap, but he wrapped one arm around her waist and held her tightly to him. She glared at him, but he only smiled back.

"Then this morning," Steve continued, "I found Mandy in one of the upstairs bedrooms. She was just standing there."

Bliss sat perfectly still, hardly breathing. Do not think, she told herself. Do not think about the heat emanating from Dutton's body. About his tantalizing aroma. About the incredibly rock-hard muscles of his thighs. She wasn't going to think about any of those things. She was going to listen to Steve's tale of woe and pretend she was sitting on a chair. Oh, ha!

"Mandy said," Steve went on, "in a wistful, funny-sounding voice, that the room would make a wonderful nursery for our baby. I nearly fell over."

Dutton pressed his hand against Bliss's stomach, his fingertips inching upward to rest just beneath her breasts. Her eyes widened, but she didn't move.

"She said she was thirty-one years old, and her biological clock was ticking, or some damn thing like that, and she wanted us to have a baby."

Dutton's hand stroked slowly back and forth in a steady, maddening rhythm, not quite touching her tingling breasts. She narrowed her eyes and wiggled her bottom closer to him. She felt more than heard his sharp intake of breath. She wiggled again.

His hand stilled. "Stop that," he whispered in her ear.

"You reap what you sow," she whispered back, out of the corner of her mouth.

"A baby," Steve said, shaking his head.

Bliss stiffened, then relaxed. "Oh, you and Mandy. Yes, a baby, of course. That's what Mandy wants. That's really so sweet."

"Are you listening to me?" Steve asked. "Or are you too busy doing whatever the hell you're doing over there?"

"We're just sitting here," Dutton said, "hanging on to every word you're saying. Right, Bliss?"

"Oh, right, right. Steve, do you really hate the idea of having a baby, being a father? I mean, really hate it?"

"I don't know," he said, throwing up his hands. "I never thought about it. Mandy and I had never discussed it. I'd mapped out our plans for traveling for the business."

"Aha!" Bliss said, pointing a finger in the air. She wiggled again, and a groan rumbled in Dutton's chest. "*You* mapped out the plan? You and Mandy didn't sit down and do it together?"

"Well, not exactly. I made it up in a report form so

I could present it to Mom and Dad. I showed it to Mandy when I finished it. She said . . ." He stared into space. "I don't remember what she said. I was hyped about showing it to Mom and Dad so they could approve the traveling expenses. We're hitting the road right after New Year's. Or we were. At the moment, Mandy isn't even speaking to me."

Dutton pressed his hand against Bliss's stomach again. "A man who fathers a child knows he'll leave a part of himself behind when he dies. That baby says the man existed, counted for something. Not everyone is meant to be a father, mine being a classic example, but you, Steve? You're sort of nuts, but you're a decent human being, a good person. Think about it, buddy. Think about watching Mandy's body change, grow big with your child. You two would have created a miracle together because of your love."

Bliss turned her head to stare at Dutton. An ache gripped her throat, and unexpected tears burned at the back of her eyes.

Such beautiful things he was saying, she mused. A baby, a miracle, created by the love of two people. Where Dutton's hand now rested on her stomach a baby would grow, nestled safely within her until he was ready to face the world. A little boy with Dutton's dark hair and eyes—Oh, heavens, where was her silly mind taking her?

Steve lunged to his feet, strode into the bathroom, and returned wearing his jacket.

"Steve?" Bliss said.

"Thanks. I really appreciate your help," he said, heading for the door. "I'm a stupid jerk, a total geek. I've got to get home and talk to Mandy. A baby. Yeah, we're going to have a baby." He left the apartment.

Bliss stared at the door for a long moment, then slowly turned her head to look at Dutton.

"Did you . . . did you mean what you said to Steve?" she asked softly. "Or were you just making it up?"

"I meant it, but I didn't realize I felt that way about a baby until I opened my mouth and started to talk about it."

"Oh."

"I've just never had any reason to think about it, I guess." He paused. "Until now." He glanced at his hand that was still splayed on Bliss's stomach, then met her gaze again. "Until now. Damn it, Bliss, what in the hell are you doing to me?"

Four

What was *she* doing to Dutton McHugh?

To Dutton McHugh, what was *she* doing?

Turning the question around this way and that did nothing to make the answer any clearer to Bliss.

She was the one who kept going off on mental tangents regarding Dutton. She'd sat there on his lap and imagined the darling baby boy they would create, their own little miracle. It was *her* mind that envisioned them making exquisite love together. Miss Stuffy and Cautious Bliss Barton making love with a man she hardly knew? Oh, good Lord.

And that was another thing that didn't make sense. She felt as though she'd known Dutton for a very long time. Perhaps it was because she'd heard Steve's stories of their reckless capers, but somehow she didn't think so. The Dutton she knew was the one she'd opened her eyes to find next to her in bed.

It was *that* Dutton who had stirred unknown desire within her, who had touched her and made her feel more feminine and alive than ever before. It was *that* Dutton who had given her a glimpse of his lonely childhood, and revealed in an unguarded moment that he liked the idea of belonging to a real family like the Bartons, if only for a couple of weeks. It was *that* Dutton who had told his best friend what it would mean to create a child with the woman he loved. *That* was the Dutton she knew—and had known, it seemed, for a long and glorious time.

What was *she* doing to Dutton McHugh?

She had no idea. But what was becoming clear, Bliss realized, was that *she* was growing closer, inch by frightening inch, to falling in love with Dutton.

"Bliss?" he said, pulling her from her reverie. "You're a million miles away."

"Oh, I'm sorry." She slid off his lap, and busied herself straightening her sweater. She straightened it some more, then a tad more.

Dutton got to his feet. "What's wrong?"

"Nothing," she said, not looking at him. Only the fact that if she fell in love with him, it would be the worst mistake of her life. Only the fact that he was a temporary visitor, and wasn't even her type in the first place. Only the fact that she was a breath away from bursting into tears, and she didn't have the foggiest notion why. "Not a thing is wrong."

"You're perfectly calm, right?"

"Calm? Oh, certainly. That's what I am. Calm. I intend to have my say about this computer nonsense, but this isn't the time because that's not your fault. You happen to be the person who is supposed to computerize me, but it wasn't your idea, so there's no sense screaming in your face about it."

"I see. So, you're calm. There's nothing else on your mind to cause you any upset."

"Nope." She patted the waistband of her sweater.

"Damn it, Bliss, you're doing it again!"

She jerked in shock at his suddenly loud voice, then spun around to face him. "What are you talking —no, yelling about?"

"Whenever you don't want to square off against something, you hightail it behind your wall of calmness. You just ignore the issue, plant a pleasant little smile on your face, and hide. Well, that isn't going to work with me, Bliss, because you're dealing with a pro who knows all about drawing invisible lines that no one can step over. They serve well, the walls, the circles, but, damn it, not this time!"

"Quit hollering at me! I don't know what you're talking about. You'd make a terrific Barton, Dutton McHugh. You're a borderline cuckoo. I'm not hiding from anything."

"Aren't you?" he asked, his voice suddenly very low and quiet.

She wrapped her arms around her waist and lifted her chin. "No."

Dutton looked at her for a long moment, and she held his gaze, ignoring her trembling knees.

"There's an old man," he said, his voice still low, "who fishes off a pier near where I live. I wander down there sometimes, and we talk about this and that. He's a widower with no children; he's all alone. He asked me once why I lived alone, when I had a choice, a chance, to share my life with someone. I just dusted him off, said my life was set up exactly the way I wanted it. He looked at me and said, 'Son, people who are lonely build walls around their hearts, instead of bridges.' I just chalked it up to an old man's ramblings and forgot it . . . until now."

"Dutton, I—"

He raised a hand to silence her. "Bliss, I can't, won't pretend that nothing is happening between us. Whatever this is, it's very different from anything I've experienced before. It's confusing, presents a whole slew of questions that I don't have the answers to. I'm not stepping into my safe circle and staying put. Bliss, don't you want to know too? Won't you come out from behind your wall, drop your phony calm facade, and find the answers with me?"

She tightened her hold on herself.

"Maybe it's nothing," he said, dragging one hand through his hair. "Just physical attraction . . . hell, lust. I don't know. Bliss, I've always been alone, and

I decided a long time ago to leave it that way. But now I keep hearing the echo of that old man's words. What if . . . what if you and I are lonely people, and because of your wall and my circle, we haven't left any room to—to build bridges? Don't hide, Bliss, not from this, not from me."

Tears misted her eyes as she stared at him. In the dark depths of his eyes, she could see the vulnerability he was willing to risk revealing to her. He had stepped out of his safe circle to find his answers, while she hid behind her wall like a frightened child.

A sob caught in her throat as she took a shaky breath. It was too much, too fast, she thought frantically. Her well-ordered life was being hurled helter-skelter into a wild wind that was sweeping it out of control. She couldn't deal with all of this at once. It was too much, too much.

Was she lonely? She didn't know. Did she, unknown even to herself, yearn to build a bridge from her heart to another's? Did she want to make her wall crumble into dust? Yes, she had questions about the new and wondrous sensations and emotions she'd felt since meeting Dutton. But did she have the courage to seek the answers? She didn't know.

And, oh, dear God, what if one of those answers was that she was falling in love with Dutton McHugh?

Temporary Dutton. The wrong man, who could shatter her heart into a million pieces.

Two tears slid down her cheeks.

"Damn," Dutton muttered as he closed the distance between them. He wrapped his arms around her and held her tightly in a warm, comforting embrace. "I didn't mean to make you cry. I never want to make you cry. I just said what I was feeling, what needed to be brought out into the open. This is heavy-duty stuff for me, and *I'm* one of the go-with-the-flow group. I'm starting to realize what this must be like for you. You're scared to death."

"Yes," she said, resting her head on his strong chest. "I can't think. I feel as though I can't breathe. It's too much, Dutton, don't you see? Maybe I *am* lonely, but if that's true, at least it's familiar, it's mine, I know how to deal with it. So much is happening so quickly, and I can't sort it out, understand it, find a place to put it all."

"Yeah, I understand, I really do. I feel like a confused mess myself, and there's usually little that throws me." He gently gripped her shoulders and moved her slightly away from him. She looked up at him. "We'll take it slow and easy. I just have to know that you're not going to be hiding behind that wall of yours. We'll find the answers together about what's happening between us. Together, Bliss. Okay?"

And if the answers didn't match up, Bliss wondered. What then? Dutton could discover that his attraction for her was only physical. He'd snap his fingers and say, "Well, son of a gun, it was pure and simple lust after all," and that would be that.

And her answers? What if they added up to the fact that indeed, she had fallen in love with Dutton

McHugh? Fallen in love with a man who would quickly grow tired of her cautious nature and need for stability and order in her life.

No, she decided. This was a no-win situation, one that she had no business in. It wasn't where she even remotely belonged. Whatever the answers were, it didn't matter, because the man was Dutton, and the woman was Bliss, and it was all totally impossible.

Still, she thought suddenly, for two weeks Dutton could be hers. During the holidays, as her private Christmas present to herself, Dutton McHugh could be hers. Even if he realized during these two weeks that his attraction to her was just physical, he'd agreed to stay until after the wedding to play his part in the charade.

It wasn't a no-win situation after all, she mused. She was guaranteed two weeks with a precious gift, Dutton. She wouldn't be seeking any answers, merely savoring each memory, knowing she would have to give her gift back when time ran out. She was a Christmas Cinderella.

"Bliss?"

"What? Oh sorry. I was thinking. I had to sort this through a bit."

"And? Will you do it? Will you give us a chance to find out what's happening here, find the answers?"

No, she thought. *She* didn't want the answers. "I won't hide behind my wall, Dutton," she said softly. Not during her magical two weeks.

"Good." He smiled warmly at her. "If someone had

told me a few days ago that I'd be in the middle of a situation like this, I would have said that person was nuts. Your family thinks we've done the ever-famous 'it' and have fallen madly in love, and they're thrilled out of their socks because they assume we'll reach the natural conclusion fast and get married. You and I are in a different place, trying to figure out what's really happening between us. This is very complicated."

"Just a tad," she said, managing a small smile. And to top it off, she had her own plan, known only to herself. "Dutton, could we put all of this on hold for now and go buy a Christmas tree?"

He framed her face in his hands. "My lady, we will find the most beautiful, absolutely perfect Christmas tree in the city of Denver for you."

"For us. It will be *our* tree."

He gazed at her for a long moment, then brushed his lips across hers. "Go bundle up. It's really cold and windy out there."

"Okay." She smiled brightly at him, her blue eyes dancing with excitement, then turned toward her bedroom.

Dutton watched as Bliss disappeared into the bedroom, and a frown clouded his features. McHugh, what are you doing? he asked himself. There had been a tight knot of fear in his gut that hadn't disappeared until Bliss had agreed to all that he'd said, had assured him that she'd come out from behind her wall and seek the answers they needed.

Why was he doing this? Why was it so important? He didn't know. He knew only that he'd never wanted any woman with such a burning, raging ache of desire as he did Bliss Barton.

It was crazy. He'd been knocked for a loop by a pint-sized woman with sparkling blue eyes and wild auburn curls. He felt disoriented, confused, and yet he'd been astonishingly relieved when Bliss had said she wouldn't hide behind her wall. It was ridiculous. Really, *really* crazy.

"I'm ready, Dutton," Bliss said, coming back into the room. "I brought you your jacket. Oh, I adore wandering through Christmas tree lots. They smell so good, don't you think?"

He shrugged. "I don't know. I've never been in a Christmas tree lot." He smiled at her. "I'll make it a point to check out the smell first thing."

"Didn't they put up Christmas trees in the foster homes?"

"Yeah, sure, but I wasn't allowed to touch them. I'd get up one morning and there would be a tree, but it never seemed to have much to do with me. Bliss, I really don't like to talk about my childhood, because I'm sure it sounds as though I'm feeling sorry for myself. I'm not. I've been an adult longer than I was a kid. I don't dwell on those early days— there's no point to it. I'm a thirty-two-year-old man now."

"Who's still alone," she said quietly. She shook her head. "I'm sorry. I shouldn't have said that. You had no control over your childhood, but your being alone now is by your own choosing. I can remember Steve's telling my mother that he didn't want to hear one word about how it was time he thought about getting married and settling down. The silly part was, my parents wouldn't have dreamed of nagging him about such a thing, but Steve figured they were due to start in on the subject. He said he was alone and doing fine, having a high old time."

Dutton smiled. "Then along came Mandy, and that was that. Wild and rowdy Steve Barton is about to be married and has a mortgage. And I'd say it would be safe money to bet there will be a Barton baby on the scene by Christmas next year. Just goes to show you, Bliss, that we never know what the future may bring. How we feel about something today isn't necessarily etched in stone."

She opened her mouth, realized she had no idea what to say, and snapped it closed again.

He chuckled. "Come on. We've got a Christmas tree to buy."

Nearly four hours later, Bliss was thoroughly convinced that her feet were blocks of ice that would never defrost. Her nose was a cold, forgotten entity somewhere in the center of her face, and tucking her gloved hands under her armpits was no longer warming her icicle fingers. She stood in yet another Christmas tree lot, hopping from one frozen foot to the other, watching her breath billow out in white puffs like smoke from a chugging train.

She'd created a monster, she thought. To turn Dutton McHugh loose in Christmas tree lots was to witness the emergence of a certifiable lunatic. When he'd declared that they'd find the most perfect Christmas tree in Denver, he hadn't been kidding. For a man who had never chosen a tree before in his life, he certainly knew what he wanted. Or, to be more precise, what he refused to settle for. He was driving the lot attendants nuts, and turning her into a human popsicle.

"Listen, Mac," the salesman said to Dutton, "so the top of the tree is a little crooked. Cut the damn top off and you won't have to see it. The rest of the tree is a beauty. They don't come no better."

Dutton rubbed his hand over his chin and squinted at the top of the tree. "I don't know."

"Dutton," Bliss said through chattering teeth, "the man has a point. We have to cut some off the top anyway, so we have room to put the angel."

Dutton shook his head. "I don't know."

"You're right, lady," the lot attendant interjected quickly. "What's a tree without an angel on the top? A sad-lookin' tree, that's what. Just whop off that crooked little bend there and you're in business."

"Well . . ." Dutton said slowly.

"Sold!" Bliss yelled.

"I don't know," Dutton said.

"Oh, hell," the man muttered.

"Dutton, please," Bliss moaned. "I'm freezing to death, and I'm hungry, and it's snowing so hard that the streets are going to be treacherous to drive on, and—and I want to go home. It's a beautiful tree. A wonderful tree. The most magnificent tree I've seen in my entire life. I love that tree, I want that tree." She paused and took a deep breath. "Let's buy the stupid tree!" she yelled.

Dutton stared at her wide-eyed, then turned to the other man.

"We'll . . . um, take the tree."

"Bless you, lady," the man said. "I hope Santa brings you a bunch of great stuff this year."

She already had her Christmas present, she thought wistfully. There he stood, the Christmas tree connoisseur of Denver . . . Dutton McHugh.

When they returned to the apartment, Dutton nodded absently as Bliss announced she was going to take a hot shower and defrost her frozen body. He was thoroughly engrossed in studying the four disassembled pieces of the tree stand, mumbling under his breath as he examined each section. Bliss swallowed a bubble of laughter and went into the bedroom.

She stayed in the shower longer than she normally would, but the hot water streaming over her felt so heavenly, she was reluctant to leave. At last convinced she was warm again from head to toe, she dried, and put on a fresh bra and panties, and a royal blue velour caftan. Deciding that her red and green striped slippers clashed horribly with the pretty robe, she padded barefoot into the living room. She stopped, her eyes widening in surprise.

"Oh, Dutton," she said, "you got the stand together, the tree up, and the lights on. It's gorgeous."

"Not bad, huh?" he said, grinning with pride. "I think I ruined that big knife of yours when I used it to saw off the crummy crooked top of the tree, but I'll get you a new one. This is really a kick, you know? Did you notice how evenly the lights are placed? I switched a few of the bulbs around too. There aren't two of the same color right next to each other anywhere on there. See?"

"Yes," she said, smiling at him, "I see." This was going to be the best, the most precious Christmas she'd ever had. "Why don't you start putting on the ornaments? I'll make some grilled cheese sandwiches and mugs of soup, then I'll help you finish decorating. Oh, and I think I'll start a fire in the fireplace."

Dutton snapped his head around to stare at the fireplace, instant pictures flashing though his mind of kissing, holding, touching Bliss in front of a roaring fire. Of making love to Bliss, showing her the ecstasy she'd never known. He'd enter her slowly, gently, sheath himself in her silken heat, take them both to a place that she didn't even realize existed. He'd—

"Dutton? Don't you want me to make a fire?"

"I'll do it! I mean, the fire. That's the 'it' I'll do. I'll light it right up. You bet."

Bliss frowned and cocked her head to one side. "Is something wrong?"

"No, no, not a thing. You go ahead and fix the food. I'm really hungry, now that I think about it. I'll get the fire going, then start putting the ornaments on the tree."

"Okay." She looked at him for another long moment and started toward the kitchen. "It won't take me long to fix the soup and sandwiches. Oh, wait." She walked over to the stereo. A few moments later, a Christmas carol floated through the air. "There. That's the final touch, really sets the mood." She turned and left the room.

Dutton groaned. "Soft nostalgic music," he muttered. "Oh, good Lord."

He shook his head and hunkered down in front of the fireplace. As he busied himself layering paper, kindling, and three logs on the grate, he decided there was a good chance he wasn't going to survive the rest of the evening. The heat that would soon leap from the roaring fire couldn't possibly be more intense than that which was beginning to consume his body.

Bliss. Lord, how he wanted her.

He struck a match and set the flame to the paper. He watched, nearly mesmerized, as the fire caught, spread, created great, licking orange flames that burned higher and hotter . . . hotter . . . hotter . . .

He closed the screen over the fire, realizing it was little barrier between him and the heat. As small a barrier as the soft blue robe Bliss wore.

She'd looked so cute out in the snow, he mused, staring into the flames. She'd stood in the Christmas tree lots with her red nose and pink cheeks, the snowflakes sprinkling over her like lacy crochet. He'd dragged her halfway around the city to find the perfect tree—their tree—until she'd had enough and exploded with a burst of that passionate temper of hers. Oh, she was something, his sweet Bliss.

And now she no longer looked cute. "Cute" had been peeled away with the bulky, snow-laden clothes, and she'd emerged from the bedroom "beautiful." The rich blue gown beckoned to him, and he yearned to run his hands over the soft material, feeling Bliss's gentle curves beneath. He'd pull her close and claim her lips, tasting her sweetness as their tongues met in the darkness of her mouth.

Then, just as he'd imagined it, he'd skim the blue robe from her lissome body, and in the glow of the flames he'd—

"Are you ready?"

He started at the sound of her voice, and turned his head to see her standing near him holding a tray. She placed it on the coffee table, then sat down on the sofa, facing him and the crackling fire.

"You certainly know how to make a fire," she said, smiling.

So did she, he thought dryly. His hands on his

thighs, he pushed himself to his feet. The fire burning deep inside him threatened to engulf him, rage out of control at any given moment. *Easy, McHugh.*

Bliss's breath caught as Dutton straightened and looked down at her. The fire behind him outlined his body, making him appear even bigger, stronger, more powerfully masculine. Shadows flickered across his face, and it was impossible to clearly see his features and figure out what he was thinking.

But she knew, could sense that he was gazing directly at her, his dark eyes seeming to sear through the caftan, sending heated sensations along her skin. Her breasts ached, desire thrummed deep within her, as she gazed up at him, etching every magnificent inch of him in her mind and heart for all time.

The silence in the room was broken only by the snapping and crackling of the fire. Another entity wove through the air, a sensual tension that seemed to draw them together.

"Our supper," Bliss said, hardly recognizing the husky quality of her own voice, "is getting cold."

"What?" He shook his head slightly. "Oh, sure." He moved around the coffee table and sat down next to her on the sofa. "This should really hit the spot. It looks good." And Bliss smelled so good, he thought, so feminine and sweet. And she was so damn beautiful. He had to concentrate on grilled cheese sandwiches! "Hungry?" He reached for a sandwich.

"Oh, yes," Bliss said, picking up half a sandwich.

She took a bite, chewed and swallowed, and wondered absently what it had tasted like.

They sat staring straight ahead into the fire, not speaking as they ate, both surprised when the soup and sandwiches were suddenly gone.

"Oh. Would you like some more?" Bliss asked. "Or maybe cookies . . . ?"

"No, no, I've had plenty. It was delicious, and I thank you."

"I'll just take this tray into the kitchen."

"Bliss, wait." He grasped one of her hands as she reached for the tray, then rested their hands on his thigh. "We have to talk."

Bliss stared at their hands. Hers was nearly eclipsed by his larger one, and his bronzed tan contrasted sharply with her fair skin. She felt the strength in his hand and in his hard, muscled thigh. And the heat, always the heat, that swept up and through her, sending her heart racing.

"Bliss?"

Her eyes collided with his as she was pulled from her private reverie. "Talk? About what?"

"Bliss, I have to tell you . . ." He paused and frowned. "Lord, I've never said anything like this before in my life. Okay, here it is. You know I want you, want to make love to you. You want me, too, but it's a hell of a lot more complicated than that because you're a . . . What I mean is, you're not into casual . . . Damn." He cleared his throat. "I'm not doing very well here."

"I understand what you're saying, Dutton. I'm a twenty-five-year-old virgin, which is definitely strange. I don't have casual affairs, and my making love with someone would thus take on connotations of greater importance than is often found in today's society, because I waited so long to experience the momentous event. Therefore, much forethought must be given to the subject before we, perhaps, decide to hop in the old sack together. How's that?"

"It was rather clinical, but I guess you covered it. Now, here's the bottom line. We can't agree on this thing, Bliss, because I want you so damn bad right now that I ache."

"Oh."

"So, I'm going to have to leave it up to you. I realize that's not entirely fair, but there's no other way to handle this. I'm scared to death that I'll seduce you into doing something you'll regret later, and I can't deal with the thought of that. The decision, Bliss, of whether or not we make love is up to you. Under the circumstances, it's the only way to do this."

"Oh."

"Could you say something besides 'Oh'? I've never taken part in a conversation like this. It isn't easy for me, you know. I'm used to reading the signals sent to me and then . . . Forget that. Bliss, the decision is yours, and I'll abide by it."

"Oh. I mean, I see, yes, I understand, Dutton. If we're to make love, I'll have to speak right up and state my business in no uncertain terms, just whip it right on you." She nodded. "Okay, I get it. I could say something like—"

He groaned. "Please, don't practice. I can't take anymore of this subject at the moment."

"Oh."

"Let's decorate the tree." He released her hand and got to his feet. "I swear, that is the best-looking Christmas tree in the city of Denver."

"*Our* tree."

"Yes," he said, smiling and extending his hand to her. "It's our tree, sweet Bliss."

Five

By late morning of the next day, Bliss had to stifle the urge to scream in frustration. Dutton was sitting behind her desk at Barton Property Management, flanked by Steve and her father, Sam. Bliss sat in a chair by the office door . . . fuming.

How dare they plow through her bookkeeping records without so much as a by your leave, she raged. How dare they treat her like a speck on the wall, instead of the person in charge of this department? Just who in the blue blazes did those three yahoos think they were? She had personally developed and implemented the record-keeping procedure for the company. It was intricate and sophisticated, the monthly statements sent to each client precise and accurate. Yes sir, that was one top-of-the-line, state-of-the-art, complicated, genius-level system they were mumbling about over there. And, by gum, it was hers!

"Seems simple enough," Dutton said. "This is a very basic setup really. The rents are paid directly to you, you send the client a statement each month with a check, minus your commission and any maintenance or repair costs. You also subtract the rental tax if the client has paid you to take care of the taxes for him. Yep, I get the picture of how it's done. Not much to it. This would be a piece of cake to put on a computer system, and the billing time would be cut by more than half. There's nothing complicated here."

"Aaak!" Bliss screamed, and jumped to her feet. The three men jerked in surprise and stared at her. "That does it." She marched across the room, eyes narrowed, teeth clenched. "Nobody is touching my records, do you hear me? My *complicated* records, that are kept under a system *I* devised because Bartons hate tedious paperwork. You"—she glared at her father, then her brother—"were certainly willing to have me take charge of this end of the operation. Now, without even consulting me, you're ready to turn it over to"—she glowered at Dutton—"that man, so one of his icky little computers can gobble it up. Well, ha!" She folded her arms across her breasts and poked her nose in the air. "Over my dead body you will."

Sam chuckled. He was an older version of Steve, with the same build, height, and blue eyes. His thick hair had turned from dark auburn to silver, and he had a year-round tan.

"Well, now," he said, smiling, "I didn't know you had that much spit and fire in you, honey. You holler real good when you get going, just like your mother." He whopped Dutton on the back. "Guess it took the love of a Barton-type man like Dutton here to bring out the real Barton in you. Glad to see it. Thrilled, in fact."

"Oh, boy." Dutton shook his head. "Dive for the foxholes."

"Bliss, what is your problem?" Steve asked. "This is going to save you hours of work every month. I'd think you'd be pleased to know that you'll have free time for"—he slid a sly glance at Dutton—"other endeavors, shall we say?"

"Dig us in a little deeper, why don't you?" Dutton muttered.

"Get . . . out . . . of . . . my office," Bliss said, her voice low and menacing. "All three of you . . . March. Exit. Disappear." She waved her hands in the air. "I mean it. Go. Now."

"Yes, well," Sam said, inching around the desk, "maybe it's time for lunch. Come on, Steve, I'll buy you a hamburger. Your mother's out, so we'll put the answering machine on. That will give Dutton a chance to . . . explain things to Bliss."

"I'm out of here," Steve said, heading for the door.

Dutton lunged to his feet. "Hey, wait a minute."

"You can handle this, son," Sam said, then high-tailed it after Steve.

Dutton dragged a hand through his hair. "Well, damn."

He looked at Bliss. One foot was tapping impatiently, and he knew she was mad as hell. And beautiful. She was wearing a soft yellow sweater with a brown flared wool skirt that gave glimpses of her shapely calves. Her auburn curls were a silken tumble, and her cheeks were flushed with anger. Absolutely beautiful.

How, he wondered with amazement, had he survived the night before without passing out on his face, or throwing Bliss down on the carpet in front of the fire and ravishing her? The hours they'd spent together had been heaven and hell, sweet torture.

The Christmas tree was a masterpiece, worthy, he'd decided, of gracing the pages of *House Beautiful.* They'd hung the ornaments together, and he'd continually filled his senses with Bliss's delicate aroma, which intertwined with the fresh smell of the pine tree.

Along with the ache of desire within him, there had been a foreign sense of inner peace. Decorating a Christmas tree was a tradition for her, something she'd done every year for all of her life, but it was a new experience for him, which he'd enjoyed from start to finish.

The long hours of the night spent tossing and turning on the sofa hadn't been a thrill a minute, though. He'd chastely kissed Bliss good night on the forehead, not daring to pull her close to his aroused body. Yet she had been there in the morning, along with their splendid Christmas tree with the angel on top.

Dutton pulled his mind back to the present and wondered how long he'd been standing there traipsing down memory lane. He should be concentrating on the fact that he'd been deserted by the Barton troops, left to deal alone with one very angry woman.

"Bliss," he said, "I realize you're angry, and I don't blame you. This wasn't handled well at all. We just stormed the gates of your domain like the gestapo. You're due an apology, Bliss, and I, for one, am sorry."

She spun to face him, her eyes flashing. "Don't you dare be understanding and sweet and say kind things to me. I'm furious beyond belief, and I intend to stay furious. If you utter one word to me about how I should calm down, I swear to heaven, McHugh, I'll punch you right in the nose. I mean it. Don't be nice."

Dutton laughed.

He certainly hadn't intended to laugh, having learned at least a meager thing or two about women over the years, but he simply couldn't help himself.

The burst of laughter had been unexpected, and prompted by the absolutely enchantingly beautiful picture Bliss presented in her fiery anger, along with the endearing lack of logic in her tirade. It was laughter born of joy more than amusement, over the fact that Bliss Barton was one hundred percent woman.

His woman. Forever.

Forever?

His laughter stilled, his smile faded. Was this it? he asked himself. Was he falling in love with Bliss? Had he, like Steve, met the one woman who would change the course of his life?

"Oh, you're infuriating," she said, then turned and marched toward the door.

"Whoa." He strode around the desk and caught her by the arm halfway across the room. He stepped in front of her, blocking her path, and placed his hands on her shoulders. "I wasn't laughing at you, Bliss."

"Oh? That's strange," she said stiffly. "It would appear that we're the only two people in the room, sir."

"Look, I laughed because . . ." He shook his head. "No, I think I'd better leave that alone for now, because I don't understand it myself. The subject here is computerizing your work system. I really am sorry it was handled the way that it was, but you know your family. They just plow in and do it when something seems like a good idea."

Bliss sighed, feeling drained as her anger ebbed. "And they know *me*. They're right, you know. I would have fought this every inch of the way if I'd been consulted about it before you arrived. I don't like change, unexpected upsets in my life. While I was growing up, I never knew what zany idea I'd find in the works when I walked into the house. My father went out once and bought tons of camping equipment. Off we went, not one of us knowing the first thing about camping. It was a disaster, and I hated it. My parents and Steve thought the whole thing was a lark, catastrophes and all. That's just one example out of a multitude of examples."

"I understand. But listen to me a second. This time they're not shooting in the dark. The bookkeeping system you've devised is sharp, right on the money. Barton Property Management has outgrown it, that's all. The company is simply too big to do it all by hand anymore. Your system can be shifted very easily onto the computer. I'll teach you how to run the machines, and you'll save countless hours every month. No, your family didn't handle the decision of going on computer with any finesse, but the bottom line is that it's a sound plan. Don't fight this, Bliss. You're the one who's going to benefit from it."

She stepped back, forcing him to drop his hands from her shoulders. Walking to the window, she stared out at the snow-covered city.

Darn that Dutton McHugh, she thought. Oh, he was a Barton clone, all right. He simply had another method of attack from the rest of the clan. While they ran roughshod over her feelings and opinions, Dutton snuck his way past her defenses with gently spoken words, and warmth radiating from his fudge-dark eyes. And once again she'd throw up her hands in defeat and go along with the majority. Her life, any decisions she might have made, had been snatched from her control. Again.

But there was one secret section of her life that was truly hers, a portion that she alone knew of. Her precious treasure that was tucked safely away from the world, her Christmas present, Dutton McHugh.

She turned to face him. "Yes, all right. Dutton, we'll go on computer. No fuss, no muss. I've never liked those machines, but I'll work on my attitude and try to be a receptive pupil." She smiled. "What an adventure I'm undertaking. Bliss Barton is about to become computerized. When do we start?"

Something wasn't quite right here, Dutton thought. It would appear that Bliss had done an about-face, had recognized the practicality and sound reasoning of using a computer for her work, but her sudden acceptance was jarring, just didn't feel right. What was going on in that beautiful head of hers?

"I'll go see the computer dealer in this area who cooperates with my firm," he said. "In fact, I'll do that right now, unless you'd like to go out to lunch first."

"No, you go ahead. I'll get a sandwich when Dad and Steve get back. Don't forget that we're expected at my parents' house tonight for their annual holiday buffet. My mother is Christmas shopping now because she turns over the house to a caterer. Her philosophy is that a person shouldn't exhaust herself preparing for a party because she'd be too tired to enjoy it. So, she shows up just like a guest."

"Sounds like a good idea."

"I suppose, but I enjoyed fixing the refreshments for Steve and Mandy's party. Well, never mind. There's no use dwelling on yet another difference between me and my family. The list contains subjects from the mundane to the major. If I'm not here when you get back, I'll meet you at the apartment."

He nodded. "Fine. Bliss, am I missing something? You switched gears so fast on this computer thing that . . . I don't know, you're awfully calm now." He crossed the room to cradle her face in his hands. "Talk to me."

"Are you afraid I'm retreating behind my wall of calmness?" she asked quietly, looking directly into his eyes.

"The thought did occur to me."

"No. No, I'm not doing that." She smiled. "I've accepted the idea of the computer system." Accepted it, then dismissed it from her mind, because there were more important things to think about. Holiday cheer and lacy snowflakes, glittering Christmas trees and wonderful presents. And Dutton. "Just don't expect me to grasp the concept of how to work the little machines in record time."

"Don't worry about a thing," he said, lowering his

head toward hers. "I'm extremely patient, and I'm a *very* good teacher."

Oh, she just bet he was, Bliss thought, seeming to float up and away as his lips touched hers. Dutton McHugh was capable of teaching her anything he put . . . his . . . mind to. Anything, and everything, and . . .

The kiss was fire. Flames licked through them every bit as hot as those that had glowed and burned in the hearth the night before. Their tongues met, darting, dueling, dancing, as desires soared as high as the leaping flames.

How did a man know, Dutton wondered hazily, if he was in love? When did the new and confusing emotions stop churning in a tangled maze and become clearly defined? And what if this really was the beginning of love? Did he *want* to be in love, be committed to another person for all time? And what of Bliss? What were her feelings for him? What did her increasingly passionate responses to his kiss and touch mean?

He lifted his head and stepped back, dropping his hands from her face. She slowly opened her eyes to meet his gaze, and saw the frown that knitted his dark brows.

"You don't appear very happy," she said uneasily. He studied her for such a long, silent moment, she frowned too. "Dutton?"

"I don't like unanswered questions, Bliss," he said, a slight edge to his voice. "I deal in facts, adjust easily to whatever comes into my life, good or bad, once I know what I'm dealing with. I learned that as a kid, because I never knew when I was going to be shuffled around. Once I was told, I just went with it, did the old go-with-the-flow routine."

She nodded, wondering where Dutton's words were headed, and what had caused his sudden mood switch. Men, she decided, were very complicated creatures.

"The attitude of 'if it feels right, do it' that Steve and I had—still have at times, I guess—is dealing in facts, if you stop and think about it. The fact being that it feels right, so . . . Cripes, I'm not making any sense." He looked up at the ceiling for a long moment, then met her gaze again. "Why are you frowning like that?"

She shrugged. "Because you are. One minute you were kissing me, then you weren't kissing me and had turned into a crabby apple."

"Well, dammit!" he yelled suddenly. "I want some solid facts here. The unanswered questions about what's happening between us are driving me crazy. *I want answers!*"

"Well, don't look at me, McHugh," she said, none too quietly. "I don't have them. You act as though this is a game, like hide-and-seek or something, and I'm hiding what you're seeking . . . or whatever."

"This is most definitely," he said, his voice now low, "not a game."

Yes, it was, Bliss thought. Sort of. The charade

they were performing for her family was a game. Her self-indulgent two weeks of having Dutton as her Christmas present was a fantasy, a game. When he left her and Denver, she could only hope he didn't pack up her heart and take it with him.

"Bliss, are you even listening to me?" he asked.

"Yes, of course I am. I just don't know what to say, except that I'm sure you'll find your answers, because you won't rest until you do."

"Aren't they *our* answers?"

"Well . . ."

"Didn't you say you'd come out from behind your wall to discover what's happening between us?"

"Dutton, please, we've been over all this."

"Bliss, you don't like change, don't like your life being pulled off course. How can I be sure that you'll face and accept the facts, the answers, when we find them?"

"I'll deal with them, Dutton," she said quietly. She already had. It was settled in an orderly fashion in her mind. The only missing piece to the puzzle was whether she was falling in love with Dutton. She didn't know, and didn't want to know.

"Yeah, well, I'd better get going," he said. "Your father is eager to have the equipment set up in here. Bartons certainly like to do things on the spot." He shook his head. "Steve has been like that ever since I've known him. Your father shows that the trait doesn't diminish any with age."

"I know," Bliss said, with a sigh. "I imagine you enjoy working and being with people like that."

"Sometimes. There are things that should be taken slower, though. Sam Barton is assuming I'll bring in the best computer for the job at the most reasonable price. I'll do exactly that, yet I'd prefer to present a report, document my findings and reasoning. But he's the boss, so I'll have the machine and printer in here by closing time today, though this is not how I like to do business."

She looked at him in surprise. "But you're like Steve. What you're saying doesn't fit the mold."

"Bliss, I'm like Steve only when it affects me and me alone. The things that Steve and I did together fell into that category. I don't run my company like that. I have a staff, people counting on me to do things in a proper manner so that their futures are secure."

"Oh, I see. I guess I just assumed that you thought like the Bartons in all areas. You know, like Steve deciding he and Mandy should travel to find new clients without really discussing it with her."

"No. Steve chose to be Mandy's other half, part of their 'we.' I personally feel he didn't handle that whole thing well with her, although it's none of my business. Granted, I answer to no one concerning my own life as long as my actions don't affect anyone else, but if I was ever committed to someone I . . . Well, enough said. I'll see you later." He brushed his lips over hers. "Bye."

"Bye," she said softly, watching as he strode from the room. She pressed her fingertips to her suddenly throbbing temples.

Darn that Dutton, she thought. What he had just said was a piece that didn't fit into the picture she had of him. He was confusing her more, it seemed, every time he opened his mouth and gave another glimpse of who he was.

If he was ever committed to someone . . . she mused. No, she mustn't dwell on that, place too much importance on those words. The truth of the matter was, he was alone by choice. The answers he sought regarding the two of them were haunting him only because he didn't have them yet. He was still closer to being a Barton than she would ever be. And she'd do well to remember that.

Bliss sighed again, then turned to watch the snow falling beyond the window.

Outside, Dutton met Steve in the parking lot.

"Where's your dad?" he asked, shoving his already cold hands into his pockets.

"He saw some buddies of his at the café where we had lunch. They're sitting around shooting the bull. Did you get Bliss settled down about the computers?"

"Yes. I'm going now to arrange for the system I feel is best for this operation."

Steve punched him on the arm. "I knew you could handle Bliss. She drives me nuts sometimes because she's so darn set in her ways."

"Well, you could have discussed this with her, Steve."

"What was the point? You saw her reaction. She wasn't having any of it. This worked out perfectly. In fact, the whole thing blows my mind. Dutton McHugh is in love with my baby sister. Unreal. You'll teach her how to loosen up, go with the flow. I love Bliss, don't ever doubt that, but she is so hung up on having things stay as they are. No changes, no upset. You've got your work cut out for you, buddy, but you'll show her the light." He looked up at the sky, whistled, and said, "All this snow. Maybe Mandy and I will take off for a couple of days and go skiing."

"It's the beginning of a work week."

Steve shrugged. "So? That's the beauty of working for a family business, one of the perks. My folks take off whenever the mood strikes. We cover for each other. Bliss is the only one who schedules her vacations."

"So do I."

"Really? Why? You're the boss of your outfit. You can do whatever you want to."

"No, I can't because . . . Forget it. I don't think you'd understand." Dutton paused. "Tell me something, Steve. How did you know you were in love with Mandy?"

"The same way you know you're in love with Bliss, I suppose."

"Humor me. Spell it out."

"Well, I don't know, Dutton. I realized I wasn't interested in seeing anyone but her. I felt very . . . possessive of her, and I didn't like other guys gawking at her too much. She was mine, and I was protecting her in a way. When I was with her, I didn't want to leave. When I was away from her, I was counting the hours until I could see her again. She became . . . a part of who I am. Hell, this is hard to explain, and it sounds ridiculous."

"No, it doesn't," Dutton said quietly. "Feeling protective, possessive, wanting her . . . It all makes sense."

Steve grinned. "What are you doing? Conducting a survey?"

"No, just looking for some answers. I'll check in with you later."

"Sure. I'm going inside. It's freezing out here, but it's great skiing weather. See ya, Dutton."

Steve sprinted into the building as Dutton walked slowly to his rented car.

Feeling protective, possessive, he mused. Wanting to be with her, not wanting to leave. A part of who he was. And the need, the burning ache to make love with Bliss, to be one with her. To hold her in his arms and never let her go.

"Oh, Lord," he muttered, yanking open the car door. Was this it? Was he in love with Bliss Barton? He slid behind the wheel, pulled the door closed, then smacked the steering wheel with the palm of his hand. "Dammit, am I? Why don't I know the answer?"

With his jaw tightly clenched, Dutton drove away, forcing himself to concentrate on maneuvering the car on the slick, snow-covered streets.

At seven o'clock that night, Dutton stood staring at the glowing Christmas tree in Bliss's living room. They'd met at the apartment, and Bliss had told him to use the bedroom first to get ready for the party. He'd showered, shaved, donned a dark suit and white shirt, and added his red tie as his token acknowledgment of the Christmas season.

He wore that tie to work one day each year near Christmas to give the impression that he was caught up in the festivities like everyone else. No one knew that Christmas came and went with his paying little attention.

Not this year, though, he thought, running one hand down the bright tie. There he stood in front of a Christmas tree that he'd helped decorate, with Bliss. He was going to the Bartons' annual Christmas buffet, with Bliss. Through the entire holiday season he wouldn't be alone because he would be with Bliss.

His gaze slid to the cold fireplace. He was not, he told himself firmly, going to replay in his mind the enticing scenario of making love to Bliss in front of the fire. The mental image of it was becoming pure torture, causing his body to tighten instantly.

He forced himself to switch his gaze back to the

tree, nodding in approval at its perfection. Bliss had taken as much time as he to carefully place each ornament according to size and color. A guy like Steve probably stuck things here and there, finished the project in fifteen minutes, and went on to something else.

Strange, Dutton mused. The Barton family considered him to be like them, fitting in with their attitudes and outlooks better than their loved but out-of-it Bliss. He was beginning to see that he was somewhere between Bliss's regimented thinking and the go-for-it philosophy of the other Bartons. He and Bliss were not total opposites, not by a long shot. Did Bliss realize that? Or did she still view him as a carbon copy of her brother?

He heard the click of the bedroom door opening and turned as Bliss entered the living room.

"Dear Lord," he said, under his breath.

He was aware of the thudding of his heart as it beat wildly, and was unable to tear his gaze from her.

Sweet Bliss, he thought. Beautiful Bliss. She was a Christmas Bliss in a full-length green velvet dress with long sleeves and a draped neckline. The soft material hugged her slender body and flared slightly as it fell to her feet. Her auburn curls were a glorious halo around her face. Exquisite.

"You are," he whispered, "the most beautiful Christmas angel I've ever seen."

"Thank you, Dutton," she said, smiling at him. "You're very handsome in your finery. I like your tie.

If I'm a Christmas angel, then you're a Christmas present."

He grinned. "Care to unwrap me? That's what you do with Christmas presents, you know."

"Yes, I know," she said, her smile wavering a bit. But she was going to have to give this Christmas present back, she reminded herself. She forced that unpleasant thought away and batted her eyelashes at him. "I'll give that unwrapping routine careful consideration, Mr. McHugh."

He laughed with delight at her exaggerated flirting. "You do that, Miss Barton."

"We'd better get our coats on and go. The roads will be slippery, and it will take longer than usual to drive to my parents' house. I hope you enjoy the party, Dutton. It's really quite a gala affair."

"I'm looking forward to it, Bliss. I'll be the envy of every guy in the place because I'll be with the beautiful Christmas angel. I'll get our coats."

And she'd be with her Christmas present, Bliss thought, a gentle smile touching her lips. Her wonderful Dutton McHugh.

Six

While Dutton had not given any particular thought to the type of home the senior Bartons might live in, he was not prepared for the enormous three-story structure, ablaze with light, that greeted them.

Set back from the road with expensive cars lining the circular drive, the house reminded Dutton of a Southern mansion that had been transported to the snowy fairyland of Denver.

"Nice little place," he said, chuckling.

Bliss shrugged. "My parents attitude of 'if it feels right, do it' paid off handsomely in many ventures in the past. That shivering young man over there will park your car."

Inside the house, uniformed attendants disappeared with Bliss's and Dutton's coats. The pair were greeted by a beaming Jenny Barton and whisked into a large living room that was jam-packed with people. A huge white Christmas tree filled one corner, decorated with red and green velvet bows, tiny white lights, and red china apples.

"I like our tree better," Dutton whispered to Bliss.

"Me, too," she said.

A lavishly catered buffet lined one wall of the living room, along with a bar serviced by a tuxedoed man. The formal dining room had been stripped of furniture, and a five-piece dance band played beckoning music.

The mood was festive, the multitude of people laughing and talking loudly. Steve and Mandy waved from across the room, then were swallowed up by the crowd. Bliss led Dutton toward the buffet, and they were stopped often by people greeting Bliss. She introduced Dutton to everyone, and he soon gave up the attempt to remember names.

They ate standing up, trying to balance their plates in the jostling crowd. They were only too happy to relinquish their plates to a passing waiter the moment they'd stopped eating.

When Bliss sighed Dutton looked down at her questioningly. "Yes?"

"I hate this thing. Every year I invent a list of dread diseases I've fallen prey to so I can't attend. Then I lose my nerve and show up."

Dutton laughed. "Bless you, sweet Bliss. I was just wondering how soon I could suggest we get out of here without hurting your feelings."

Her eyes widened in surprise. "You? But . . . Steve loves this affair. He's always one of the last to leave. I can remember him telling my father that you and he hit every party you could find in San Diego when you were in the navy."

"Come on," Dutton said, gripping her elbow, "let's dance."

"But—"

"Shh."

They inched their way across the living room to the dimly lit dancing area. The band was playing a dreamy waltz, and the room wasn't overly crowded.

Dutton drew Bliss into his arms, luxuriating in the feel of her slender, velvet-clad body against his. Her dress had a deep V in the back, baring a portion of her smooth skin. He stroked his hand across that skin, nearly groaning at the exquisite sensation. Say something, he told himself, before you take her right here on the dance floor.

"Bliss," he said, moving back so he could look at her, "I want you to listen to me."

"What is it?"

"I am *not* Steve. I haven't been in the navy since I was twenty-five. Yes, I have a social life in San Francisco, but I'm not the party animal you seem to think I am. I don't drop everything and go skiing, or sailing, or whatever, because I have a business to run. Yes, I like to think I'm adaptable to change, to whatever curves life tosses me. Steve is my best friend. We have a lot in common, and we've been in and out of scrapes together. But, Bliss, I'm not a carbon copy of a Barton. I'm me, Dutton McHugh, pure and simple, and it's time that you realized that."

"But—"

"Shh. Just think about what I said." He pulled her close again and moved her slowly across the floor in time to the music.

Well, for Pete's sake, Bliss thought, what a bossy man. He delivered a startling speech, then didn't even let her comment. Not that she would have known what to say. She'd resigned herself to the fact that Dutton was a Barton clone. Now he'd muddled her brain with the declaration that he was not an exact reproduction of Steve Barton. Dutton had seemed to be saying he possessed only some of the Barton traits. Did that mean he was capable of understanding and sympathizing with some of her fuddy-duddy tendencies?

Dutton pulled her closer to avoid bumping into another couple, and as her breasts were crushed against his hard chest, she totally lost her train of thought.

She'd think about all of this later, she decided. Her mind now refused to go beyond recognizing anything other than the heightened awareness of her senses, and the desire pulsing deep within her.

Oh, the incredible heat, and power, and gentleness of Dutton. She was wrapped in the heavenly cocoon of his strong embrace, her body molded to his, and the music floating through the air was being played just for them. Yes, she'd think later. For now, she wished only to feel.

She snuggled closer to him.

Heaven help him, Dutton thought, gritting his teeth. Dancing with Bliss had not been a terrific idea. All his stern commands to his body to remain in control were being totally ignored. The blood was pounding in his veins, heat was gathering low and heavy within him, sparking the now familiar ache of desire.

Bliss sighed, a contented, sensual-sounding sigh, and he rolled his eyes heavenward.

Think about something, McHugh, he told himself. He had to concentrate on something other than the delectable creature in his arms and what she was doing to him physically. Okay, he was thinking. No, he was dying. Lord, how he wanted this woman.

The song ended, and a new one started almost immediately, another slow, dreamy tune.

What he should think about, Dutton decided, was his grand speech about his not being a Barton replica. It had suddenly seemed vitally important that Bliss understood who and what he was, and—even more—what he wasn't. Right now, though, he didn't care if she understood. He knew only that if she didn't stop wiggling against him, he was going to explode!

"Bliss," he said, his voice hoarse, "let's get out of here."

"Hmm?" she said dreamily. "Oh. Certainly, Dutton. I'm ready to go home any time you are."

Home, she thought. That sounded lovely. She would go home with Dutton, and they'd shut the door on the world.

Home, Dutton mused, with Bliss. Lord, that had a nice ring to it. Oh, for cripes sake, he was getting ridiculously sentimental and romantic. No wonder he'd always ignored the holiday season. It turned a man into a mush-brain who got caught up in traditions and Christmas trees and fireplaces. Fireplaces? *Can it, McHugh.* He wasn't starting that torturous scenario rolling through his mind again. No way.

It was over a half an hour later before Bliss and Dutton managed to drive away from the Barton home. They had worked their way across the crowded living room to find the senior Bartons and say good night, received and ignored a knowing wink from Steve as they collected their coats from the attendants, then escaped at last into the snowy night.

A howling, whipping wind accompanied a fresh snowstorm that had just arrived in Denver, and neither spoke as Dutton concentrated on driving. The roads were slick, the windshield wipers labored under the heavy, wet snow, and the going was slow.

Bliss sat quietly in the passenger seat, lost in her own thoughts and nearly oblivious to the raging storm outside the car.

Home with Dutton, her mind echoed. This night, this magical night, was theirs.

She turned her head to look at Dutton, who was bent slightly over the steering wheel, straining to see the road beyond the windshield. Excitement tingled through her, accompanied by frissons of heat. Her gaze slid over his body from head to toe, missing no detail, loving all that she saw. Her perusal halted on his hands, tightly gripping the steering wheel.

Beautiful hands, she mused. Large, tanned, powerful hands. Hands that she knew would caress her bare skin with gentleness and expertise. Hands that would follow the path of where his lips had gone, igniting her passion to a fever pitch . . .

Her gaze flew to his face. She momentarily expected him to turn to her and demand to know where her sensual mental journey was taking her, them. Her heart beat rapidly as she sought the answer to his unasked question.

Tonight, she thought, a strange inner calmness mingling with her desire, she would make love with Dutton McHugh. It was a decision she knew she would never regret. Among her precious memories when Dutton left her would be this wondrous night. It was right, it was time. It was hers, and it would be forever.

She drew a steadying breath and willed her heart to slow its wild cadence. What if, she thought suddenly, because of some misplaced sense of loyalty to

Steve and her parents, Dutton refused to make love with her?

He wanted her, she knew that. It was more evident each time he took her into his arms and kissed her. He had wanted her, for heaven's sake, in the middle of a crowded dance floor! She may not be very experienced, but she wasn't exactly stupid either.

No, she decided firmly, she would not let him deny her this magical night. This night was theirs. It had to be.

"There," Dutton said, jarring her from her racing thoughts. "Made it." He turned off the ignition. "Wait until I come around for you. It's slippery out there. I don't want you to end up sitting in a snowdrift."

Heaven forbid, she thought, smiling. There was nothing seductive about a soggy Christmas angel. Her smile faded as Dutton got out of the car. Seductive? As in, seduce Dutton McHugh? Not give him a chance to be noble and courageous, and remember that she was his best friend's sister . . . and a virgin? How on earth did a person go about seducing a man as worldly as Dutton?

"Well, figure it out, Bliss," she said aloud, "and hurry up."

He opened her door and extended his hand to her. They walked carefully across the slick parking lot, and both breathed a sigh of relief when they entered Bliss's apartment.

"I'll hang our coats in the shower," Dutton said.

"Fine."

As soon as he left the room, Bliss plugged in the cord that brought the Christmas tree alive with glowing, rainbow-colored lights. She snapped off the lamp on the end table, then knelt down in front of the fireplace and set a match to the paper beneath the kindling and logs. As she got to her feet, Dutton came back into the room and stopped dead in his tracks.

"What are you doing?" he asked.

"Lighting a fire."

"In the fireplace?" He hoped his voice hadn't really had a squeaky sound to it.

She frowned. "That's the best place for a fire, don't you think?"

"What happened to the light on the end table?" he asked, yanking off his red tie. "Do you want me to change the light bulb?"

"No, I turned it off. I thought the tree would look prettier that way." Was she imagining it, or did Dutton seem nervous, tense? "Okay?"

"Yeah, sure, sure," he said, nodding. She slipped her shoes off. "Now what are you doing?"

"Taking off my shoes. They're new, and they pinch my toes. Would you like some brandy?"

"Good idea. A drink. I'll get us each a brandy for a nightcap, then we'll call it a day. Right? You bet. Fine." He turned and strode into the kitchen.

This, Bliss thought gloomily, was not going well. Apparently Dutton was going to bring her a grown-up drink, pat her on the head like a child, then ship her off to bed. Alone. Well, ha!

She crossed the room to turn on the stereo, then hurried back to the sofa as soft music began to float dreamily through the air. She sat on the center cushion, deciding that Dutton would be close to her on either side.

"Here you go," he said, coming back into the room. He handed her a snifter, but remained standing. "Cheers." He lifted his glass high, then took a swallow of the amber liquid.

Bliss patted the cushion to the right of her. "Don't you want to sit down, Dutton? The fire is heavenly."

The fire was in the fireplace, he thought, and that fireplace and the images it conjured up in his mind were not his best friends. The fire was matching the one gaining force in his aching body. Well, he'd just have to handle this. After all, how long did it take to drink an inch or so of brandy? He'd purposely scrimped on the servings with the plan to shuffle Bliss off to bed, alone, as quickly as possible. Then he would die in silent agony in front of that damnable fireplace.

"Dutton?"

"What? Oh." He eased himself onto the cushion next to her, careful not to brush his leg against hers. "It's warm." He set his snifter on the coffee table, stood up again, removed his jacket, and tossed it onto a chair. Then he resumed his stiff pose next to Bliss. "Better."

He sounded like a robot, Bliss thought, speaking one programmed word at a time. Oh, she was really doing a lousy job of seduction. Dutton hadn't even touched her since they'd arrived at the apartment. Didn't he want to make love with her as much as she did with him?

"Oh, dear," she said, not realizing the softly spoken words had escaped her lips.

Dutton frowned. He took her snifter and set it on the coffee table, then slipped his arm around her shoulders.

"What's wrong, Bliss?" he asked quietly. "You suddenly sound very sad."

She turned her head to meet his gaze, looking deep into his dark eyes, searching for what she hoped to find.

Yes, her heart sang, it was there. The smoldering desire was reflected in the near-ebony depths of Dutton's eyes. She could see it now, just as she had felt it earlier as they'd danced. Dutton McHugh wanted her. But Dutton McHugh also wanted answers to all the questions plaguing him about what was happening between them.

No questions, no answers tonight, Dutton, she silently begged. Not tonight, this magical Christmas night. These hours were theirs. She was his sweet Bliss, his Christmas angel, and he was her Christmas present. Nothing else mattered.

"Bliss?"

"Would you . . . would you kiss me, please, Dutton?" she asked, her voice shaky.

Oh, Lord, Dutton thought, stifling a groan. He

couldn't kiss her. He was hanging on to his control by a thread. *He wanted her so damn much.* But this was Bliss. No, he couldn't kiss her, not tonight.

She shifted slightly on the cushion and ran her hands slowly up his chest, feeling him tense beneath her palms. She laced her fingers behind his neck and leaned closer to him. Courage born of want and need, of both body and heart, surged through her.

She flicked the tip of her tongue over his lips.

"Bliss, you don't understand," he said, his voice hoarse. "I can't kiss you, because if I do . . ." Her tongue repeated the sensuous foray. "Oh my God. Bliss, listen to me." A trickle of sweat slithered down his back. His body ached. He burned like the fire in the hearth. "Listen, okay?"

"No. This time, please, listen to me," she said, close to his lips. "I'm Bliss, your sweet Bliss. I have no other name except your Christmas angel. There's no world beyond this room, Dutton. No questions, no answers, no people here. There's only the two of us, together, with our beautiful Christmas tree and the warmth of the fire. It's our night, a magical night." She drew a shuddering breath. "I want you, Dutton McHugh. I want to make love with you, and I promise I will never regret it. If you don't want me—"

"Oh, Bliss."

His mouth came down hard on hers. He gathered her close to him, his tongue plummeting deep into the sweet darkness of her mouth, finding her tongue, savoring her taste. He inhaled her delightful aroma as his hands roamed over her back, loving the feel of her skin. His arousal was instantaneous, straining against his slacks, aching for the release that only the silken haven of Bliss's body could give him.

McHugh, no! his mind roared. Why was Bliss doing this? Something in what she'd said wasn't quite right. *Think!* No world beyond this room? Yes, there was. She had no name except sweet Bliss and his Christmas angel? Yes, she did. Magical night? A fantasy night? No, this was real, didn't she see that?

But . . .

She wanted him to make love with her. He hadn't seduced her into submission, hadn't run roughshod over her ability to reason. She was coming to him as a woman.

His woman.

His sweet Bliss.

A soft purr of pleasure escaped her lips and he was lost.

He raised his head to draw a ragged breath, then claimed her mouth once more. His hands found the tiny tab of the zipper at the back of the velvet dress, and he slowly drew it down. He broke the kiss and moved back so he could see her face. She lifted her lashes to reveal eyes nearly smoky gray with desire. Her lips were moist, beckoning to him to cover them again with his own.

Good Lord, how he wanted her.

As Bliss looked directly into Dutton's eyes, she

smiled with happiness. Oh, yes, this was right. She felt no trepidation, only desire. The heat within her was consuming her. She wished only to feel, to savor all that was Dutton, all that he would bring to her. There would be no regrets, no tears, only memories, precious memories.

She pulled her arms from his neck and felt the cool air against her heated skin as he drew her dress down her arms, revealing the dark green, satin camisole she wore. The velvet pooled at her waist, then the satin as she reached for the buttons on his shirt, freeing them one by one. She brushed the material aside, sighing at the sight of his magnificent tanned chest. She tangled her fingers in the soft dark hair covering it, then leaned forward to lightly kiss what her hands explored.

So beautiful, she mused. He was just so beautiful. His skin tasted slightly salty, his aroma was heady, so male. Her breasts were heavy, aching for his touch, the feel of his hands on her soft flesh.

As though in tune with her most secret thoughts, he gently cupped her breasts, stroking the nipples with his thumbs. The sensitive buds responded instantly, hardening to taut points.

"You're more lovely than satin," he whispered. "Your skin is like ivory velvet. So soft, so lovely. Ah, Bliss, you're exquisite."

"Thank . . . thank you," she said, hardly able to breathe.

He shifted his legs as he gripped her waist, and in

the next moment she was stretched out along his rugged length on the sofa. He looked directly into her eyes for a long, heart-stopping minute, then moved her upward with effortless ease, his mouth seeking and finding one of her breasts. The nipple tightened once more from the laving of his tongue, then he drew the soft flesh deep into his mouth, suckling, pulling, savoring.

Bliss sighed with pleasure. "Oh, Dutton."

Sensations like none she'd ever known stirred within her. The heat within her seemed to scorch her as the pulsing rhythm of Dutton's mouth on her breast was matched by a tightening deep inside her. She could feel his arousal full and heavy against her, his body announcing his need and his glorious desire for her.

He moved to her other breast, and again she sighed, a purely feminine sound. She lay on his bare chest, feeling the hard muscles, the moist hair, the rapid beating of his heart.

With obvious reluctance Dutton pulled away from her breast and shifted her downward. His mouth captured hers as his fingers wove through her hair, holding her head steady to receive his delving, teasing tongue deep into her mouth. Then he released her head so his hands could roam over the dewy skin of her back.

She slowly lifted her head to meet his smoldering gaze. "Oh, Dutton, I—I feel so . . . I want you."

"No regrets? Please, Bliss, say it again, tell me

you're certain. About a million years ago, it seems, I told you that the decision would be yours, because I wanted you from the moment I saw you. But this is so damn important, for both of us, and I have to hear the words again. Tell me you'll never be sorry that you . . . that we . . . I'll be damned if I'll say did 'it.' I hate that."

She smiled. "Then I won't say the 'it' word." Her smile faded. "Oh, yes, Dutton, I'm very sure about what I'm . . . what we're doing. I've closed the door and my mind against everything except being myself, just Bliss, listening to my heart. I know I'm cautious, and I know, without any lingering doubt, that I want to make love with you. No regrets, Dutton, I promise you that. This is our night, our wonderful, Christmas angel and the Christmas present night."

He framed her face with his hands and kissed her with searing intensity. Then suddenly she was being lifted up and away. She teetered slightly as Dutton set her on her feet, and her dress and camisole slithered to the floor with a hushed swish. She stood before him in the glow of the fire and the Christmas tree lights, clad only in satin panties that matched the discarded satin camisole.

"So beautiful," he said, his voice rough.

Then he removed his clothes, tossing them onto the sofa.

Magnificent, she thought dreamily. Dutton McHugh was magnificent beyond description. The fire and

tree lights played over his burnished body, accentuating the lean muscles and perfect proportions. His
arousal was bold, announcing his virility, showing
her all that he was and would bring to her.

She stepped free of the velvet pool of her dress and
walked into his embrace, entwining her arms around
his neck and pressing her body tightly to his. Her
sensitized breasts crushed against his chest in a
sweet pain as his hands splayed on her back, then
moved lower to catch the waistband of her panties.
His kiss was urgent, frenzied, his manhood surging
against her.

Slow down, McHugh! he told himself. This was
Bliss, innocent Bliss, who was trusting him with
the very essence of herself, offering him her most
precious gift. He mustn't frighten her, and, dear
Lord, he didn't want to hurt her. She felt so small
and delicate in his arms. He had never before been
so aware of his own size and power, of the strength
he possessed that had to be tempered with infinite
gentleness. This night would be like no other, the
lovemaking shared with Bliss as special, rare, beautiful as she deserved it to be.

He lifted his head and stepped back. Brushing his
lips over hers, he slid the satin panties down her
slender legs. When he straightened, his gaze traced
every inch of her.

"Oh, Bliss, I don't have the words to tell you how
exquisite you are, how much this, what we're about
to share, means to me. I want this to be perfect for

you, but the first time isn't always that great for a woman because . . ." He cleared his throat. "What I'm trying to say is, trust me, okay? It'll get better and better, but . . . Oh, hell, I'm not doing this very well."

She smiled. "I understand. I trust you, Dutton, you know that I do." She held out her hand to him. "I'm yours," she whispered.

A fierce ache closed Dutton's throat, and he was unable to speak. He looked at the small hand Bliss extended toward him, met her warm gaze for a moment, then shifted his eyes back to her hand.

Emotions slammed against his heart and mind, spilling over one another, impossible to decipher.

He lifted one of his own hands, vaguely aware that it was trembling. Slowly he reached for Bliss's and saw, as though from a far misty distance, his large hand envelop her small one.

At that instant, the whirling emotions stilled. The questions had been answered.

He was in love with his sweet Bliss.

"My God," he said in a harsh whisper.

He tightened his hold on her hand and stepped closer, circling her shoulders with his arm to pull her near. He nestled their hands between her breasts, not wishing to break the bond, the symbol of what his hand enclosing hers represented. He buried his face in her silken hair and held her, simply held her, allowing the peace of the moment to flood through him and mingle with his raging desire.

He loved her. He, Dutton McHugh, was in love with Bliss Barton. Did he want to be a man in love, held in an emotional grip over which he had no control or defense? Oh, God, he didn't know, but he wouldn't think about that now. He was in love, and about to make love, with the woman who totally possessed his heart.

He raised his head. "Here, in front of the fire . . . we'll make love here. I'll get the quilt from your bed. I've fantasized about being with you in front of this fire, Bliss. All right?"

"Yes."

"Don't move." He turned and strode into the bedroom.

Don't move? she thought. She could hardly breathe, let alone entertain the idea that her trembling legs would support any attempt she made to walk. Oh, how she wanted Dutton. This wondrous night was suspended in another world, existed in a place far from reality. There was nothing but the two of them, Bliss and Dutton, no thoughts beyond the moment.

He returned, spread the fluffy down quilt in front of the crackling fire, then pulled her into his arms. He kissed her deeply, before laying her on the soft quilt and stretching out next to her.

The firelight danced over them, and the heat of the fire matched the inferno raging inside them.

Dutton rested one hand on Bliss's stomach and leaned over her to kiss her, his tongue meeting hers. He moved lower to suck first one breast, then the other, sweat beading his brow as she again purred in feminine pleasure.

Slow and easy, McHugh, he told himself fiercely.

Oh, hurry, please, Dutton, she begged silently. I want you so very much.

He shifted lower to kiss the place where his hand had rested, as his fingers trailed down one of her legs, then upward again. He hesitated, then sought the nest of auburn curls that hid her womanliness and her secrets.

Bliss inhaled sharply, her body tensing, yet in the next instant she relaxed again, savoring the marvelous sensations rocketing through her. "Oh, Dutton. Oh, yes, yes."

She traced the sculpted muscles of his back, then sank her fingers into his thick, night-dark hair. She was awash with desire and the increasing heat that was overwhelming her. As Dutton's hand and lips tantalized every inch of her, she tossed her head restlessly, aching with an enticing pain, needing, something she had never known but had to have. Now.

"Oh, Dutton, please," she said, a tiny sob catching in her throat.

He gritted his teeth, his muscles trembling from forced restraint, his manhood surging with the want of her.

"I have to be certain you're ready for me, Bliss," he said hoarsely. She slid her hand slowly down his glistening chest. "I won't rush . . . you . . . because . . ." Her hand crept lower. "Bliss, don't. My control is at the edge, and . . ." Gentle fingers found what they sought. "Bliss . . ."

He moved over her, catching his weight on his forearms, and kissed her.

Not yet, McHugh, he told himself.

Now, Dutton, now, she whispered silently.

He raised his head, then planted nibbling kisses along her throat and across the tops of her breasts.

"Dutton, please," she said, and lifted her hips.

The last of Dutton's control snapped.

He entered her, her liquid heat sheathing him, welcoming him. He watched Bliss's face for any hint of pain or fear, but saw none. He moved farther into her dark haven of ecstasy until he met Nature's barrier.

"Hold onto me," he said hoarsely. "I don't want to hurt you, but . . . Just hold on tight."

"Yes."

With his jaw clenched so hard his teeth ached, he surged into her, filling her. He heard her sharp gasp, then her soft sigh. He waited, gathering his last ounce of restraint to allow her body to adjust to his invasion.

Her lashes drifted down, then she opened her eyes again, wanting to see his face in the glow of the fire. They were one. The pain had been fleeting, unimportant. The essence of this man was within her, joining them, meshing them into one entity. It was beautiful, far beyond her fantasies of what this intimate act might be like.

Dutton began to move.

The tempo was slow at first, then increased as need consumed him. Bliss met his rhythm, instinct leading the way as she urged him on, sliding her hands along his back to his tight buttocks. Pressure built deep inside her, swirling in tightening circles. Dutton thundered within her, and she gloried in his power, in his strength, which was carrying her up and away as her body sought an unknown.

Sought . . . then found.

"Dutton!"

"Yes! Bliss, yes."

She was flung into an abyss of ecstasy as spasms swept through her. Wave after crashing wave washed over her, her body tightening around Dutton, drawing him even farther into her honeyed heat.

With a groan that rumbled from deep in his chest, he drove heavily within her one last time, then joined her in the place where she had gone.

"Bliss! Sweet . . . Bliss."

They were suspended in time, hovered there, then slowly drifted back to the welcoming warmth of the fire in the hearth. The room steadied, then stilled, as they returned to reality.

"Oh, Dutton," Bliss whispered. "That was so beautiful, so wonderful. Thank you. That was, you are, the most precious Christmas present I've ever received."

He gave her a fast, hard kiss. "You were sensational. Lord, I can't put it into words. Just believe me when I say that it was very, very special." And he loved her. No, he wasn't ready to think about that, not yet. "I'm going to move off you n—"

"No, no, don't leave me. I can feel you inside of me. I don't want you to go."

He smiled. "Give your body a break. It's going to be complaining a bit about this momentous event." He eased off of her, then pulled the edge of the quilt over them. "We could move to the bed, I suppose."

"Later," she murmured, snuggling closer to him. "It's so nice here in front of the fire."

"What happened in front of this fire was beyond my wildest dreams." He kissed her on the forehead. "No regrets, Bliss?"

"No, of course not," she said, her eyes drifting closed. "Mmm."

Lord, how he loved her, he thought, gazing at her face.

Then, in the glow of the fire and the rainbow of Christmas tree lights, they slept.

Seven

The following days passed quickly.

Working hours were filled with Dutton's giving Bliss instructions on the computer. He was, as he'd promised, a patient teacher. She was, as she'd promised, a willing student. But there was much to learn, and the pupil made mistakes.

"It ate them," Bliss wailed, smacking the computer with the palm of her hand. "Ow! That hurt. Dutton, did you see that? I typed in account records for the past hour and now . . . poof . . . they're gone. The stupid thing gobbled them up."

Dutton attempted to stifle his chuckle, but failed. "That happens to everyone at some time or another,

Bliss. You pressed the wrong key when you were saving the records onto the disk, that's all."

"That's all? How can you say that? I typed my little heart out for a solid hour."

"I know, I know. You go out and get us a sandwich for lunch, and I'll retype what you did."

"Fine," she said, with an indignant sniff. "I'm not bringing that—that monster a sandwich. It already ate my work."

Dutton's laughter followed her as she stomped out of the room.

The evenings were a mixture of social events for the bride-and-groom-to-be, holiday parties, and a few quiet evenings spent talking, reading, or watching the many holiday programs on television. Bliss and Dutton shared the cooking and cleaning up, along with the chores around the apartment.

And the nights. The nights were lovemaking in Bliss's bed, or in front of the fire. The nights were ecstasy as Bliss and Dutton reached for each other eagerly, burning with a desire that never died, but remained like the glowing embers in the hearth, just waiting for the slightest touch or brush of lips to ignite the flame of passion. The nights were lovemaking that was alternately slow, sweet, and sensuous, and fast and urgent.

The night before Steve and Mandy's wedding, which would take place the evening of December twenty-third, Dutton sat alone in Bliss's apartment. They'd attended the wedding rehearsal the previous night, and now Bliss was at yet another bridal shower for Mandy.

Dutton had been at Steve's bachelor party earlier in the week and had, to his own amazement, not particularly enjoyed himself. The volume of noise, the mandatory off-color jokes, the endless flow of liquor, had not been for Dutton a fun, all-male outing. Even the scantily clad girl who had popped out of a cardboard cake had been, in his opinion, a disappointment. She had been, in no uncertain terms, fat.

Dutton sat slouched on the sofa, his fingers laced loosely on his chest, his long, jean-clad legs stretched out in front of him and crossed at the ankles. He stared into the crackling flames of the fire, a deep frown on his face.

His time in Denver had seemed to fly by, he mused, one day rolling into the next so quickly, it was hard to keep track of what day of the week it was.

He pushed himself to his feet, put another log on the fire, then resumed his slouched pose on the sofa.

On the surface, he knew, the days and nights spent with Bliss had been sensational, perfect even. He could talk to her about all and everything, no subject too mundane or controversial. They laughed and loved together, and he felt as though he'd known her for a lifetime.

And he loved her.

With every passing day and night, he loved her more.

That was what was brewing below the surface of their tranquil existence, he admitted. Not once during the time they'd spent together had they addressed the subject of their feelings, or the future.

He had, at first, struggled with one last question— did he want to be in love with Bliss Barton?

The answer had come, though. When he looked at her, heard her laughter, saw her smile, woke up next to her in the morning, he knew. When he weighed what he was sharing with her now against his hollow, lonely existence in San Francisco, he knew. When he gazed at their Christmas tree, then envisioned future Christmases without her by his side, he knew.

Oh, yes, he was in love with Bliss. But even more, he *wanted* to be in love with her, marry her and spend the remainder of his days with his sweet, sweet Bliss.

So, why hadn't he told her? he asked himself. That was an easy question to answer. He hadn't told her he loved her, hadn't asked her to marry him, because he was scared to death of what she would say.

She kept calling him her Christmas present.

There was something about the way she said it, he'd realized several days ago, that set him on edge, caused a chill to slither down his back. It was difficult to define, but she seemed to be reminding him of the time limit on their relationship whenever she called him her Christmas present.

"Damn," he muttered.

He straightened and leaned forward, resting his elbows on his knees and making a steeple of his fingers as he continued to stare into the leaping, orange flames.

There were other clues as well, he mused, that made him feel things were a step off the track, not quite right.

Bliss mentioned too often that he was more of a Barton than she. She seemed determined to remind him continually of their differences in personality, outlooks, lifestyles. When he'd told her that he pictured himself in the middle of the road between the Bartons and her, she'd looked at him for a long moment, then finally shaken her head and changed the subject.

Dutton got to his feet and began to pace the floor. Questions were piling up again, he realized, and he had no intention of repeating that emotional turmoil. He was also running out of time. He was scheduled to return to San Francisco the day after Christmas. The countdown was on, the hours remaining with Bliss measured off in rapidly decreasing numbers.

Enough was enough, he decided firmly. He was going to sit Bliss down, tell her that he loved her, ask her to marry him, and pray to heaven he'd imagined that their relationship was slightly out of kilter. Yes, he was going to do it. Tonight.

As if his decision had conjured her, Bliss entered the apartment at that moment.

"Hi," she said as she took off her snow-covered coat. "Oh, I'm frozen. I'll change and be right out. That fire looks wonderful."

"Did you have a nice evening?" he asked.

She started toward the bedroom. "It was all right, I suppose. Mandy got some lovely gifts, but I don't fit into groups like that very well. They were Mandy's friends, and I really didn't have anything in common with them or much to say." She shrugged. "Oh, well, it doesn't matter. I'll be back in a second."

In the bedroom, Bliss quickly changed into her robe and slippers, then stepped in front of the bathroom mirror to brush her hair. She flicked the auburn waves into place, then lowered her hand, staring at her reflection.

How strange, she thought. Every time she looked at her reflection she fully expected to see on her face the changes that had taken place within her mind, her heart, her very soul. But staring back at her was simply the familiar Bliss she had always known, exactly the same.

She knew, though, she was changed forever, not remotely close to who she had been the morning she'd opened her eyes and discovered the horrors of her first hangover. And discovered Dutton next to her in bed. From that moment forward she had stepped into a world she'd never dreamed would exist for her.

She gripped the edge of the sink and leaned toward the mirror for a closer inspection. No, none of it showed. Not the warm glow within her whenever she saw Dutton, heard his voice, his laughter. Not the flush of desire that heated her cheeks whenever he drew her into his arms. Not the sated contentment after their beautiful lovemaking.

Not the fact that she was deeply and forever in love with Dutton McHugh.

Bliss pressed her fingertips to her lips and drew a wobbly breath, willing herself not to cry, not to give way to the tears that now continually hovered so near the surface.

When, exactly, had she fallen in love with Dutton? She didn't know, and it didn't really matter. What was true, and couldn't be ignored, was that it had happened, she'd fallen in love with him.

And because she had, her heart was going to be shattered into a million pieces.

"Darn you, Bliss Barton," she whispered to her reflection. Dutton was to have been only her Christmas present, a temporary, precious gift. She had mentally organized and planned the scenario, realizing it was emotionally risky, but confident that her cautious nature and sense of order would keep her on the right track.

She hadn't known about the magnitude of the power of love. She hadn't known it would overwhelm her like a giant wave. She hadn't known about the threatening tears and the ache in her heart that might consume her even before Dutton was gone.

She walked slowly back into the bedroom, practicing bright smiles as she went. Dutton would never know of her love for him, she vowed. She had promised him that she'd have no regrets about her decision to live with him and make love with him.

The days and nights they'd shared had been glorious. She had been sweet Bliss, Dutton's Christmas angel, not Bliss Barton trying to appease her family. What she'd done had been for herself, and for that she would never be sorry.

But, oh, dear God, she hadn't intended to fall in love with him, a man more like a Barton than she herself. He wasn't a Barton clone, as she'd first thought, for Dutton had tempered some of his wilder impulses. He was a free spirit nonetheless, a man who lived alone by choice. A man who would pack his suitcases and return to San Francisco, taking her heart with him.

Yes, she loved him, but he would never, ever know.

She squared her shoulders, lifted her chin, and went into the living room. Dutton was standing in front of the fireplace, his hands shoved into his pockets as he stared at the leaping flames. Bliss stopped, her heart beating wildly as she looked at him.

Magnificent Dutton, she thought. How empty this little home of hers would be without his vibrant presence. Everywhere she turned within these rooms there would be memories, bittersweet memories.

As if sensing she was there, Dutton turned to face her. "Bliss," he said quietly, "I'd like to talk to you."

"Oh?" she said, forcing a smile. "You sound so serious. Did I gum up something on the computer again?"

"No. You're doing very well on the computer—you know that." He pulled his hands free of his pockets and swept one arm in the direction of the sofa. "Why don't you sit down?"

"Sure." She settled onto the sofa and looked questioningly at him. "What is it, Dutton?"

"Time has passed very quickly since I arrived in Denver."

"Yes it has. We've been so busy. Don't you want to sit down?"

"No. Time has passed, and a lot has happened between us."

"That's true," she said, nodding. They'd made love, and she'd fallen in love. Oh, Dutton.

"Bliss, you know I'm scheduled to return to San Francisco the day after Christmas."

Yes she knew that! She didn't need to hear it, his words hitting her painfully like stones. Why was Dutton talking about this? Where was this conversation leading? She wanted to run to her bed, pull the blankets over her head, and cry. The tears were now only a breath away. She had to end this discussion as quickly as possible.

"I know when you're leaving, Dutton," she said, hoping her voice was steady. "I can take care of telling my parents that we decided we were incompatible, simply couldn't live under the same roof.

Let's see . . . I could deliver a message to Steve from you, saying that you'll be in touch soon. That should cover it." She faked a yawn, patting her hand over her mouth. "My, my, I'm sleepy. I think I'll go to bed earlier than usual tonight."

A knot tightened in Dutton's gut with such sudden force, it felt as though a knife had been plunged into him, causing momentary excruciating pain.

They were true, he thought. His worst suspicions about his and Bliss's relationship were true! He'd been her Christmas present, a temporary lover whom she'd had no intention of dealing with beyond the holidays. All they'd shared meant nothing to her. She was dusting him off, breezily waving good-bye. He'd be out of sight, out of mind, just as the ornaments on their Christmas tree would be when she packed them away. Dammit, no!

"Incompatible," he repeated, a muscle jumping along his jaw.

"Well, yes, that's what we agreed upon at the onset. You know, to explain why we were no longer together. And"—she would *not* cry—"and it's true, Dutton. I mean, we've had a marvelous holiday, but it's been a social whirlwind, not anything like the way I usually live my life. I live very quietly compared to the other Bartons. I follow a routine because I prefer it that way. I don't 'go with the flow' very well. You do, I know that, and I couldn't begin to keep up with you or . . . All I'm saying is that telling my parents that we're incompatible isn't a bold-faced lie."

"So that's it?" he said, his voice rising. "The day after Christmas you just chalk us up, end of story? Dammit, Bliss, hasn't this meant anything to you? I was your Christmas present, right? That's what you keep calling me. What did you ask Santa Claus to bring you? A stud who would relieve you of your socially unacceptable virginity?"

Oh, Lord, he thought in the next instant, what a rotten thing to say. He hadn't meant that! He was striking back at Bliss because he couldn't handle his own emotional pain and his shattered dreams.

The color drained from her face, and a sob caught in her throat. "Is that what you think?" she asked, her voice trembling. "That I used you? That I used you to . . ."

"Bliss, no, I didn't mean . . ."

She fought against her threatening tears. "Yes, I can see where you could very well think that, Dutton. I made it plain that when I was with you, I was going to do what *I* wanted to, not what was expected of me by my hopeful parents and brother, who were cheering in the wings because you had come into my life and would pull me from my fuddy-duddy cocoon."

Tears slid down her cheeks.

"I told you that when we were together, Dutton, nothing existed beyond our door, that I was only Bliss, your sweet Bliss, your"—she dashed the tears from her cheeks, but more followed—"your Christmas angel. And I realize that I called you my Christmas present many, many times."

"Bliss, please don't cry." He took a step toward her.

"No," she said, shaking her head. He stopped, dragging a hand through his hair in frustration. Bliss got shakily to her feet and looked at him. "What I shared with you was done by my own choosing. For the first time in my life I wasn't seeking the approval of my family. I was doing what I wanted to do. If that's using you, Dutton, then I'm guilty as charged. I wanted to make love with you, and I have never—and will never—regret that decision. A decision, I might add, that had nothing to do with getting rid of my virginity."

"Dammit, Bliss, I know that. I shouldn't have said what I did. I didn't mean it, I swear it. It's all been piling up, nagging at me. The things you said, your calling me your Christmas present, all of it, kept warning me that there was a time limit on what we've had together here."

"There is," she said, confused by his words. "We knew that from the beginning. The day after Christmas you'll get on a plane and leave. You *were* my Christmas present, Dutton, don't you see? After Christmas it's over." Tears now flowed unchecked down her face. "It's . . . over."

He closed the distance between them and gripped her shoulders. "Why?" he asked, nearly yelling. "Why does it have to be over? Can you really seal all of this up in a capsule and shove it away somewhere, vaguely remember it every now and then as that interesting little interlude at Christmas time with what's-his-name?"

"Don't make me sound so cold and clinical," she said, matching his rising volume. "I'm facing the facts as they are. Bartons don't always do that. They just plow ahead with their often misplaced sense of adventure, and let the chips fall where they may. Surely you understand that theory, Mr. Barton-type Man. Well, I'm Bliss, and I don't conduct my life that way. What I do with the memories of our time together is nobody's business but my own. The Christmas holidays end . . . and so do we. And that, Dutton McHugh, is how it is."

She pulled free of his grasp and stepped back, swiping at her tears. Lifting her chin, she met his gaze directly, hoping she'd achieved the blank expression she was striving for.

Oh, God, Dutton, her heart and mind cried, *I love you.*

"Well, that's clear enough," he said, his voice low and strangely flat. "You certainly stuck to the original plan, didn't you? But then, why should that surprise me? You're orderly and organized—everything in its proper place, operating on your schedule. You stepped out of your routine only because you wanted to, and gave yourself a Christmas present. Me. When Christmas is over, you'll have no further use for me. I understand. I guess I just lost it for a while, got caught up in the holiday season, the atmosphere it creates that I've never experienced before. Don't worry, Bliss, I'm back on track now. Most definitely back on track."

He turned and walked to the fireplace, stopping with his back to her, staring down into the leaping flames.

Well, he thought ruefully, he'd salvaged a shred of his pride, at least, by not acting the fool and blurting out that he loved her. But his hopes and dreams, fantasies and plans, for a future with Bliss were gone, crushed into dust. He had been Bliss's Christmas present, nothing more. God, that hurt. He loved her, had wanted to spend the rest of his life with her, but she . . .

He stared up at the ceiling for a long moment, attempting to hold together his splintering emotions. He felt hollow, empty, and terribly cold. The flames of the fire did nothing to warm the icy fist of loneliness within him that was growing larger with every beat of his heart. And every tick of the clock, which measured off the remaining hours before he boarded that airplane, disappeared into the clouds and out of Bliss's life. Forever.

He turned slightly to look at the glowing Christmas tree, his gaze lingering on the delicate gold angel on the top. A dark cloak of depression dropped over him as he realized he'd never felt so alone in his entire life.

• • •

Bliss once again wiped the tears from her cheeks, knowing there were many more to come. They would flow unchecked during the long, lonely nights after Dutton was gone.

It had all come apart, she thought dismally. Her present had been snatched from her before Christmas. How foolish she'd been to believe that memories of Dutton would be enough to sustain her through the days, the years ahead. How naive to think that she could share with Dutton all that they had and not fall in love with him. And now the piper wanted his due. She would pay, with her endless tears and shattered heart.

As she gazed at Dutton, fresh tears blurred her vision, blending everything together. Dutton was intertwined with the lights of the Christmas tree, as though he were standing in a waterfall of colors. He seemed a mythical creature, a giant of a man, strong and big and dark, transported here from a land of fantasy.

In a way, that was true, and soon he would return to the place where he really belonged.

In fairy tales and fantasy legends, she mused, there was often a magic potion, or special, secret words that would change the make-believe creature into a human form able to love the one who loved him, stay forever by that person's side.

Bliss blinked against her tears, trying in vain to

separate Dutton from the fountain of colored lights pouring over him.

If she spoke her secret message, she wondered, told Dutton of her love for him, would he stay with her for all time? Would they suddenly be able to erase the word "incompatible" from their vocabulary? Would he turn into a homebody, content with quiet evenings, instead of the whirlwind of social events they'd attended since he'd arrived in Denver?

No.

She sighed. Her declaration of love would serve no purpose other than to portray her as a textbook case of the once-innocent convinced that she was in love with the first man with whom she'd been intimate. If she flung herself into Dutton's arms and spilled out her feelings for him, she would accomplish nothing more than to make him uncomfortable, and thoroughly embarrass herself, as he fumbled for something to say in reply.

He would, she surmised, tell her that she, like him, had been caught up in the romantic holiday atmosphere. He'd simply "lost it," as he'd put it, but had been quick to regain control. He once again had the facts, the glaring facts, of their incompatibility. Their time together had been temporary.

They had little in common, except for the most beautiful lovemaking imaginable.

And that wasn't enough.

"I'm very tired, Dutton," she said, hearing the threat of tears in her voice. "I guess I'll go to bed.

There really isn't any more to be said. If you're willing, we'll continue with our original charade as planned. I'd hate to cast a gloomy mood over Steve and Mandy's wedding, or Christmas itself. It will just be a few more days, then you'll be free to—to go." She paused. "All right?"

He turned to face her, no readable expression on his face. "I'll carry out my end of the bargain. After all, this charade was my idea in the first place. No one will see any difference in our behavior between now and when I . . . when I leave."

"Thank you."

He ran his hand over the back of his neck. "Bliss, this conversation has brought to the surface the truth of the charade we're acting out. I know I left the decision of our lovemaking to you, and what we've shared has been . . ." He cleared his throat and took a deep breath before speaking further. "I think it would be best if I slept on the sofa from now until I leave."

No! his mind roared. He didn't want to give up one precious moment with Bliss. But he couldn't handle it, couldn't handle making love with her, sleeping with their heads resting on the same pillow, waking at dawn to make slow, lazy love again. He couldn't do it, knowing his time with Bliss was ticking away.

"I see," she whispered. Oh, no, she thought painfully. They'd be a room apart, a world apart. It wasn't fair, it wasn't time. He was to have been hers until

Christmas. "I—I understand. I must get to bed. I'm terribly tired. Good night, Dutton. There are extra sheets on the shelf in the closet by the door. I hope . . . you sleep well." She turned and nearly ran into the bedroom.

Dutton watched her go, silently telling her he loved her. Then he shifted his gaze to the Christmas tree, standing motionless as he stared at the delicate angel glittering on the top.

Eight

Steve and Mandy had decided on a small chapel wedding with mostly family in attendance, to be followed by a huge reception in the ballroom of one of Denver's most luxurious hotels.

There were a dozen people in the candlelit chapel, including Mandy's parents and her two brothers. Poinsettias sat in vibrant splendor on the altar, and garlands of pine edged the pews, filling the air with their sweet aroma.

It was, Bliss thought wistfully, absolutely beautiful. It was a perfect combination of Christmas and the serenity of the chapel. The candlelight was a lovely finishing touch, with tall red and white candles standing in a majestic row across the altar.

Bliss felt strange, as though none of this were quite real. The perfection of the setting made her feel she'd been dropped into the center of a painted picture. But then, she'd felt strange ever since her discussion with Dutton the night before.

He'd been gone by the time she got up that morning. He hadn't appeared at the office by the time her father had closed up at noon in honor of Steve and Mandy's wedding. Back at the apartment, she'd found a note from him saying he'd meet her at the chapel.

And there he was . . . Dutton McHugh. He was the best man, resplendent in his dark suit with the festive touch of a red rose in his lapel. And she was the maid of honor, his counterpart, for this special ceremony. Her crushed velvet street-length dress was Christmas red, which should have clashed terribly with her auburn hair, except that Mandy had found the perfect shade.

The minister's words were a distant hum, like the buzzing of bees, as Bliss looked at Dutton from beneath her lashes.

Oh, how she loved him, she thought. The flickering candlelight accentuated the angled planes of his handsome face and the night-darkness of his hair. It brought back memories of their beautiful lovemaking in front of the crackling fire and—*Bliss Barton, shame on you.* That was definitely not what one should be dwelling on in church.

But how could she not think of Dutton and all they'd shared? How could she push those memories into a dusty corner of her mind and forget them? How could she ignore the ache of tears in her throat, and ignore that magnificent man standing a few feet away from her?

A few feet? No, a world away. His body was here, but Dutton's mind was probably already in San Francisco. What they'd had for stolen days and nights was over.

She felt the tears burning at the back of her eyes and pulled her gaze from Dutton. She stared at Mandy and Steve, willing her tears not to spill over, willing her heart to quiet its wild, painful cadence, willing her mind to halt its continuing, tormenting echo of her unspoken declaration of love for Dutton.

I, Dutton, take you, Bliss, to be my lawfully wedded wife, Dutton's mind whispered. *Oh, McHugh, knock it off.* He was torturing himself, fantasizing that this storybook-perfect setting was for him and Bliss.

He should be marrying his Christmas angel now, right there in that festive yet ethereal chapel. He should be pledging his love to Bliss for all time, and hearing her repeat her own vows. They should be beginning their life together as husband and wife.

Instead Bliss had mentally put him in a Barton slot and turned the key to lock him in place. She was standing across from him looking so beautiful in the candlelight, and so damn calm. She had, no doubt, retreated behind her protective wall, where he could never again reach her.

What should he have done differently during their time together? he asked himself yet again. What could he have done to show Bliss, prove to her, that he wasn't, as she put it, a Barton-type man in every sense of the word?

He'd been fighting the preconceived ideas she had of him from the stories Steve had told over the years of his best friend. He'd had two strikes against him before he'd even gotten up to bat.

And he'd lost.

Damn, he thought, how could Bliss stand there looking so lovely, so serene, and so darn calm? What they had shared had been special, rare, like nothing he'd ever known before. But that was Bliss, he supposed. Orderly, organized Bliss, who had apparently already wrapped up the memories of their time spent together in a neat little package, and tucked them away somewhere in her mind.

Oh, yes, he had lost, and the emotional pain was nearly beyond belief in its intensity.

"You may kiss the bride," the minister said.

Dutton jerked in surprise, and realized he'd hardly heard a word of the ceremony. He'd managed to give the ring to Steve at the proper moment, but beyond that he'd been submerged in his own thoughts. Steve and Mandy were married, were a couple, complete. Dutton McHugh was chillingly alone.

The chapel was so small that the usual trip back down the aisle was unnecessary. The parents rushed to the couple. Hugs, kisses, and handshakes were exchanged, and everyone was talking at once. The minister beamed at the happy group.

Bliss stepped aside at the same moment that Dutton moved. Bliss bumped into Dutton.

"Oh," she gasped. "Excuse me. I'm sorry."

"No damage done," he said.

Their eyes met and held, and suddenly it seemed as though there were no one but the two of them in the chapel. They stood inches apart, not touching, yet their emotions were so intense both felt as if they were held tightly in each other's arms. Sensuality rose between them like a tidal wave threatening to carry them away.

Neither moved. The inches that separated them could just as well have been miles of an unpassable path cluttered with unspoken words and secrets.

"Let's get to the reception," Steve said.

Dutton jerked again as Steve's voice cut through the hazy mist that seemed to be surrounding him and Bliss.

Bliss blinked, then tore her gaze from Dutton to look at Steve.

Steve whopped Dutton on the back. "Hey, buddy, I saw the way you were looking at my baby sister just now. This love stuff is something, isn't it? Fantastic. You've got a case of love that's as terminal as mine, pal. You two will be the next ones picking out wedding rings." He glanced around. "Everybody ready to go to the hotel? Reverend Williams, you and your wife are coming, aren't you?"

"We wouldn't miss it, Steve," the minister said, laughing.

Everyone started talking at once again, deciding who was going in which car. Bliss tuned it all out as she stared at the bouquet of red rosebuds and baby's breath she clutched tightly in her hands. Steve's words to Dutton echoed in her mind.

Dutton had looked at her like a man in love? she asked herself. No, that was crazy. Steve was on an emotional high, seeing love in bloom everywhere he turned. Dutton wasn't in love with her. He was back on track, as he'd put it, doing nothing more than acting out his role in the charade. In love with her? No. He no longer even wished to kiss her, much less make love to her. He was in the countdown to his escape, his return to his life in San Francisco. Steve was wrong.

". . . and Bliss will ride with Dutton," she heard her mother say. "I'm sure you two want to be together. I don't know why you came in separate cars in the first place. Well, no matter. I'll drive your car over to the hotel, Bliss. I'm beyond ravishing your father in the front seat of an automobile, anyway. I'll deal with him later. There, we're all set. Let's get to this party."

"Mother," Bliss said quickly. "I can drive my own car. It's fine, really it is."

"Don't be silly, dear. You go on with Dutton. Romance is buzzing in the air after that beautiful ceremony. I wouldn't dream of separating you two even for a drive across town. Shoo. Go."

"Come on, Bliss," Dutton said, gripping her elbow. "Where's your purse? We'll give your car key to your mother and be on our way."

"Excellent," Sam said. "It takes a Barton kind of man to step in and get the job done."

Thanks for nothing, Sam, Dutton thought dryly, forcing a smile. Any niggling doubts that Bliss might have regarding his being a true-blue Barton-type man would be snuffed out by the continual remarks like that made by the Barton family. Damn. But then again, it didn't matter what the Bartons said. It was over between him and Bliss. She'd made that coldly clear.

Everyone left the chapel and climbed into their cars. Bliss was swept along, vaguely aware that Dutton still firmly held her elbow. Before she was completely sure how it happened, she was in Dutton's car and they were driving away from the church. She concentrated on her bouquet, her grip on it tightening.

The silence in the car hung like an oppressive weight.

Dutton finally cleared his throat, then spoke without looking at her.

"Nice wedding," he said.

"Yes."

"I hate those big productions some people have that are like a three-ring circus. Steve and Mandy had the kind of wedding that I would want if I got married."

Bliss nodded, still staring at the bouquet. "Yes, it was just right, really lovely. I don't care for those huge affairs either."

"Well, I'll be darned," he said, a slightly sarcastic edge to his voice. "We actually agreed on something. We have in common, it would seem, the kind of wedding we prefer."

"It's not important," Bliss said softly. Not important because the wedding, the ceremony bonding the two people for all time, would not be Bliss Barton repeating vows with Dutton McHugh.

"Isn't it?" he asked.

"No."

"Did it ever occur to you, Bliss, that we have a great deal in common? Much more than just our preference in weddings?"

"Dutton, don't. There's no point in this. Facts are facts. Please, just leave it alone."

Dutton clenched his jaw so tightly to keep from speaking further, his teeth ached. Sudden anger churned within him, intertwined with the chill of pain and loneliness. Hot anger that diminished, overpowered the icy fist in his gut. And the anger brought with it a new determination, born of frustration and fury.

Damn it to blue blazes and back, he thought fiercely. He was in love for the first time in his life. Totally, irrevocably in love with his sweet Bliss. And what was he going to do? He was going to run back to San Francisco like a whipped puppy scurrying for cover.

The hell he would!

Bliss Barton loved him!

He had lived with that woman, made love with that woman, seen the look in her beautiful blue eyes when she'd gazed at him, and the gentle smiles that made her glow. He didn't care what she said or what her attitude implied, he knew she was in love with him. She loved him every bit as much as he loved her.

And, by damn, he wasn't going to give her up without a fight!

He narrowed his eyes and tapped his fingers on the steering wheel.

This, he decided, was going to call for carefully planned, well thought-out strategy. This was going to call for patience and finesse. He was reentering the game, and he intended to win.

A slow smile crept onto his face, and he began to hum "Jingle Bells," tapping his fingers in time to the peppy holiday song.

Bliss frowned and looked over at Dutton. What on earth had gotten into him? she wondered. He'd done a sudden mood switch from nearly surly to humming "Jingle Bells"? That was definitely weird, and he was making her very nervous. What was going on in that gorgeous head of his?

"There's the hotel on the corner," he said cheerfully. "Knowing Steve, this ought to be quite a bash, a first-class party. I thought I'd had enough of parties, considering all we've attended, but the more I think about it, I realize I'm looking forward to this one. A party connected to something as special as a wedding is special, too, don't you think?"

"Well, I—"

"Now, my buddy Steve," he went on, chuckling, "doesn't think there is such a thing as too many parties. Of course, once he becomes a father, he just might change his views on the subject. People do change, you know, Bliss. Me? I haven't been to a wild party in San Francisco in . . . oh, let's see . . . it must be three months. Then I hit Denver, and you took me in hand. For a non-Barton Barton, you sure dragged me to a lot of noisy affairs."

"Me?" she said, her voice squeaking.

"I rather prefer a quiet dinner with a lovely lady, then maybe seeing some live theater or a movie. A walk along the wharf is nice, too. Peaceful, low-key stuff, you know what I mean?"

"You?"

"Sure. I work hard all week, and I like to relax in my free time. I've been known to rent a stack of video movies for my VCR, make a ton of popcorn, and settle in for the weekend. I love it."

Bliss opened her mouth, decided she'd sounded

like a squeaking mouse quite enough, and clamped her mouth shut again. She stared at Dutton with wide eyes.

Movies and popcorn at home? She adored doing that. Had done it, in fact, just last month. She had no idea Dutton would enjoy such an evening. Quiet dinners, the theater? Bypass the parties as a general rule? Dutton McHugh? No, he was kidding. He hadn't complained once about the party circuit they'd been on. Then again, he *had* been eager to escape from the crushing mob at her parents' party. But . . . Darn the man, he was confusing her, muddling her brain.

"There's a parking place," he said, and slid a quick glance at Bliss.

Good, he thought. She looked totally bewildered, with a cute little frown at her face that wrinkled her nose. He'd tried over the past days to get it across to her that he was not who she thought he was, yet everything he'd said had just bounced off her wall of preconceived notions. Well, no more Mr. Nice Guy. The game was over—this was war!

He parked the car, then came around to help Bliss out of her seat. She held her purse and the bouquet in one hand, and he took her other one, wrapping it around his arm. They started across the parking lot as light snowflakes began to fall. Dutton glanced up at the sky.

"I wonder if there will be a fresh batch of snow for

a picture-perfect white Christmas," he said, glancing up at the sky. "I can see where people might take off to ski during Christmas, but I would want to be in my own home on the big day."

"Really?" she said. "There were many years when I opened my presents in a ski resort."

He shrugged. "Well, you're a Barton."

"Oh, but I always wished I was at home," she added quickly.

"I'll start traditions," he went on, as though she hadn't spoken. "Since my Christmases as a kid were duds, I think that from now on I'm going to have special traditions. Yes, sir, this is the last Christmas I'm spending away from home. I've got the hang of picking out a tree and decorating it, so that's a good beginning."

Bliss nearly stumbled as she once again stared up at Dutton with wide eyes.

"Steve and Mandy are leaving for Aspen Christmas afternoon," she said, "after they've finished opening their gifts."

"To each his own."

"But Steve said you'd want to go, too, if it weren't for the fact that you were leaving for San Francisco the next day. He realizes that even though you and I are—are in love, you still have a business to run that won't wait. I thought he was quoting you about wanting to go on the skiing trip."

"Nope. He never mentioned it. He *assumed* I'd want

to go if I was still here, but he's wrong. Aspen on Christmas Day? No way."

"Oh," Bliss said, her mind racing. This didn't make sense. What Dutton was saying didn't fit the mold. He wanted to stay home on Christmas, establish traditions, personally buy and decorate a tree? Eat popcorn, for crying out loud? She'd had no glimpse of this side of him while they'd been living together, except for when they'd decorated their own beautiful Christmas tree.

They had spent a couple of quiet evenings in her apartment, but most nights they'd been on the go. She'd been sure that Dutton had been bored stiff on those rare occasions when they'd stayed in, watching holiday programs on television, reading, chatting. She'd soaked up, like a thirsty sponge, the peaceful hours spent with him, trying to ignore the fact that he was probably itching to be out and about, doing the town.

But now he was saying . . . Oh, drat, she fumed. Her mind was such a befuddled mess, she couldn't think straight. He'd made it clear that he didn't leave his business on a whim the way Steve did, yet . . .

"Ma'am," he said, pulling open the door to the hotel.

"What? Oh, yes, thank you."

"Is something wrong, Bliss?" he asked, all innocence. They started across the lobby to the bank of elevators. "You've been frowning a lot. You're looking forward to the reception, aren't you? You seemed to enjoy all the parties we attended, just like a true Barton. Well, you did say your folks' affair was a bit much, but surely you're anticipating a wonderful time at your own brother's wedding reception?"

"Yes. No. I mean, I'm not a Barton, Dutton. Well, I'm a Barton because I'm Bliss Barton, but I didn't enjoy all the parties. Well, I sort of did, because some were for Steve and Mandy, and there is something special about holiday activities, but on the whole I prefer . . . I don't think I'm making any sense."

They stepped into the elevator.

"No, you're not," Dutton said, patting her hand, "but you're understandably jangled. After all, your only brother just got married. That's a big event. You'll calm down. Do remember that you're a pro at being calm. Where's your ever-famous calmness, my sweet Bliss?"

Lost in the tangle of her mind, she thought bleakly. She felt like one of the computer disks when she'd tried to load too much information onto it. The computer had simply refused to cooperate. Her brain was balking at the moment, too, having been thoroughly overloaded by all Dutton was saying. Calm? Not a chance. She was a total wreck.

Why? she wondered. Why was Dutton saying all this now, when their relationship was over? What was he attempting to do just a few hours before he left her and Denver far behind? Why was he slipping in references to the fact that *she* had behaved more like a Barton these past few weeks than he? Darn it, what was Dutton McHugh up to?

She sighed and shook her head, completely confused. They left the elevator and walked down a carpeted corridor to a huge room where a rock band was playing lively music. A many-tiered wedding cake sat on a table at one end of the ballroom, the traditional white cake decorated with red sugar rosebuds. Waiters were milling among the many people with trays of bubbling champagne, and Steve and Mandy were moving through the crowd, greeting their guests. More people were arriving every minute, and excitement crackled through the air. Another table was piled high with attractively wrapped gifts in every shape and size imaginable.

"First-class, just like I said," Dutton commented.

"Yes, it all looks lovely, and everyone seems to be in great spirits," Bliss said.

"There are probably some people who are still shocked that Steve Barton actually took the big step and got married. They should know by now that you Bartons are full of surprises."

"I consider myself rather predictable, Dutton."

He raised his eyebrows. "How many people in this room would have imagined that set-in-her-ways Bliss Barton would be living with a man she found in her bed the morning after a wild party held in said Miss Barton's apartment? Hmm? Answer me that?"

The astonished "Oh" that formed on Bliss's lips never erupted as Dutton brushed his lips over hers.

"Think about it," he murmured, then grinned at her. He straightened, snagged two glasses of champagne from the tray of a passing waiter, and handed one to her. "Go easy on that stuff now. You know what happened the last time you overindulged." He winked at her, the grin widening. "Oh, but you warned me that you're predictable, didn't you? Does that mean I should expect you to get good and sloshed because you're obviously very fond of champagne?"

"No!" she said indignantly. "Don't be absurd."

He shrugged. "Just taking what you say as what you mean. The last time you were celebrating for Steve and Mandy and the champagne flowed, you drank enough to float away. So, since you swear up and down that you're predictable, and since we're celebrating for Steve and Mandy with champagne again . . ." He shrugged. "Just trying to stay on my toes. You Bartons are hard to keep up with, you know."

"Would you stop that?" she said loudly.

Several people turned to look at her and she smiled wanly at them. As she redirected her attention to Dutton, she narrowed her eyes at him. He simply smiled pleasantly. She drained her glass in two hefty swallows.

He peered into her empty glass. "Uh-oh, here she goes, folks. Predictable Bliss."

"Dutton McHugh," she whispered, her eyes flashing with anger, "shut up, just shut up. You're driving me right out of my mind."

He splayed one hand on his chest. "Me?"

"You're talking in riddles, jumbling my brain, confusing my thought processes, befuddling my mind."

"All that? I've just been chatting. I can't think of anything that I've said that isn't true. Have I ever lied to you? I would never lie to you, sweet Bliss. I can remember Steve's telling me, way back when we were in the navy, that you Bartons put a lot of emphasis on honesty. I like that, because I've always felt the same way."

"We . . . Bartons," she said weakly. She plunked her empty glass on a passing waiter's tray. "The Barton clan, all of us, me included." She shook her head. "I thought you understood that I'm not really a Barton."

He placed one hand lightly on her cheek, his smile gone, his voice gentle when he spoke. "Aren't you? Aren't you like them in some ways, but not others, which is true of any member of a family? Isn't it true of me? I've been labeled by you as a one hundred percent Barton-type man, but I'm not. I'm me, Dutton McHugh, possessing some Barton traits, but not others. You're more of a Barton than you realize, or are willing to admit."

"No."

"Oh, yes. You put the 'if it feels right, do it' theory into effect when I moved in with you, when we made love."

She looked quickly around the room. "Shh. Some-one will hear you, Dutton."

"Let them listen. Want to know what I think?"

"No."

"Tough. I'm going to tell you. I think you're stand-ing in the middle of the road, just like I am. You're part Barton, but the rest is you, a unique, lovely, special woman. I'm in the middle too. I'm a Barton in some ways, but not all. I'm myself, a man not popped out of anyone's mold."

"Why are you doing this, saying all this? Why are you suddenly so determined to totally confuse me just before you leave?" She felt the tears burning at the back of her eyes. "It's over, Dutton, between you and me. We covered that last night, remember?" Her heart was shattered into a million pieces last night, remember? "Why are you saying all these strange things now?"

"They're not strange, they're true, and they need saying. You've hidden behind your wall of calmness for so long that you've been peering out with tunnel vision. You see yourself as a non-Barton, me as a totally Barton-type man, and you're wrong. You got lost behind that wall, Bliss, didn't recognize the changes within yourself as you grew into a woman. You view everything in black and white—you see no gray, no middle ground. Well, there is a middle ground, and it's time you realized that."

"But . . ."

"That's one reason I said all these things now. The

other reason is . . ." He hesitated for a moment. ". . . I'm going to tell Steve and your parents that an emergency has come up in my business that needs my personal attention immediately."

"What—what are you saying?" she whispered.

Dutton squared his shoulders and looked straight at her. "I'm catching a midnight plane for San Francisco. I've decided that it's the best thing to do. I'm leaving, Bliss. Tonight."

Nine

Christmas came and Christmas went.

Bliss's face ached from her forced smiles. Before she had gathered her emotional courage enough on Christmas Day to tell her family that she and Dutton were finished, that they'd agreed to end their relationship because they were incompatible, her parents announced that they were off to Aspen to ski with Steve and Mandy.

Bliss had plastered on another of her smiles and wished them all a marvelous trip. No, she'd said brightly, she didn't want to go along, and she would oversee the operations at Barton Property Management while they were away.

Steve had kidded her about being glued to the telephone for what would no doubt be daily calls from Dutton, and she had fought fiercely against her always-threatening tears.

In a flurry of activity and chatter, the couples had prepared to leave on their trip, deciding not to return until New Year's Day.

Bliss went home to her apartment and, with no lovely carols floating through the air, nor a warm fire crackling in the hearth, slowly removed each ornament from the Christmas tree. With tears streaming down her face, she nestled the angel in its tissue-lined box. The building manager came and dragged the tree to the dumpster. She vacuumed up the strewn pine needles, then sank onto the sofa.

"And this," she said aloud, nearly choking on a sob, "is the sound of loneliness." She covered her face with her hands. "Oh, Dutton."

The citizens of Denver ushered the new year in with the usual fanfare. At midnight the city was alive with boisterous activity; horns were blown, balloons set free, people shouted, sang, and danced. Excitement and merriment were nearly palpable.

Bliss lay in the darkness in her bed, staring up at the ceiling, only vaguely aware of the noise and festivities beyond her window.

She had done little else than cry since Dutton had so abruptly and unexpectedly left. She'd gone through her days in a gloomy, depressed state of mind, and cried during the nights, managing only to doze off and on.

What she hadn't done was think beyond the fact that Dutton was gone forever.

"Enough of this," she said, swiping at the tears on her cheeks.

Tentatively, carefully, she mentally inched her way back to the day of Steve and Mandy's wedding. With extreme caution, she went over the strange things Dutton had said to her during their last hours together.

At the time, she realized, he'd done nothing more than totally confuse her. She suddenly needed to unscramble the puzzle. She wasn't sure why. Dutton was gone forever, yet his words that last day were like unfinished business that had to be tended to. It was a new year, and she had to move forward, somehow, for the sake of her own sanity.

She was, after all, Bliss Barton, and Bartons were strong, resilient people.

She was Bliss Barton . . . Bliss Barton . . .

She sat straight up in bed, her mind racing. She snapped on the lamp on the nightstand, threw back the blankets, and slid off the bed. Oblivious to the cold, she began to pace the floor, her flannel nightie swishing around her bare feet.

Dutton's voice was so clear in her mind, it was as though he were in the room with her, close enough to touch.

People do change, you know, Bliss . . . I haven't

been to a wild party in San Francisco in . . . three months . . . For a non-Barton Barton, you sure dragged me to a lot of noisy affairs.

Yes, she had, Bliss thought, nodding. And except for the annual event at her parents, which was just too big and crowded, she'd enjoyed every party they'd attended.

She had liked wearing her prettiest dresses and being caught up in the excitement of Christmas and the wedding. She'd laughed and chatted and be-haved like—like a Barton.

I've been known to rent a stack of video movies for my VCR, make a ton of popcorn, and settle in for the weekend. I love it.

He loved it? It was a perfect way to spend an evening. She'd done it herself on many occasions, but always alone, never dreaming that anyone would wish to join her. But Dutton McHugh would. Dutton McHugh, who enjoyed a good party, also recognized the need to unwind with movies and popcorn.

I'll start traditions . . . this is the last Christmas I'm spending away from home.

Oh, yes, she thought, Christmas at home. Not at ski resorts or fancy hotels, but at home, with a beautiful tree, the special angel glittering on the top.

As Bliss continued to pace she went over every-thing Dutton had said. She heard him say that she was a Barton in some ways but not in others, that the two of them were unique individuals who chose their own paths. She was more of a Barton than she realized, but not a carbon copy of her parents or brother. She was Bliss.

She sank onto the edge of the bed and pressed her hands to her cold cheeks. If it feels right, do it, she thought. That was one of the Barton philosophies. But she had gone one step further, she now realized, for as long as she could remember. She had finished the slogan with, "But if it feels wrong, don't."

It had, she told herself, taken as much Barton courage to stand firm in her own beliefs as it had for the others to have their go-with-the-flow attitude. She wasn't a fuddy-duddy, she was true to herself, just as all the Bartons were. That she didn't match up perfectly to the others didn't matter!

The maze of confusion in Bliss's mind unraveled like a tangled skein of yarn now smoothed and straightened. Her heart soared as she fit each piece to the puzzle in place to complete the picture.

Dutton had been right about so many things. He had seen with such wisdom and caring who she really was, while she had floundered behind her protective wall, declaring herself a misfit. He had made a supreme effort during their last hours together to show her, tell her, what she hadn't even realized that she desperately needed to know.

And then he had left her to work it all through on her own, which was the only way it could be properly done.

Why? Why had he gone to such lengths for her?

Why had he refused to stay, be her Christmas present, but instead given her the most precious gift of all, herself? Why had he subjected himself to a Christmas alone in San Francisco when she knew he'd been looking forward to joining the Barton family in their celebration?

Because he loved her.

"Oh, Dutton," she whispered, tears misting her eyes. "Yes. Yes, my love, I understand now. I'm Bliss, I'm Bliss Barton. I'm sweet Bliss. I'm me. Oh, Dutton, I love you so very, very much."

She turned off the light, snuggled beneath the blankets on the bed, and drifted into a peaceful sleep, a soft smile on her lips.

At eleven o'clock the next night, a very nervous Bliss Barton stood in a carpeted corridor, staring at the number on a door that told her in no uncertain terms that she was outside of Dutton McHugh's apartment.

She had been standing there for a full five minutes, and had the dismal thought that if she didn't gather her courage, she'd be there for another five minutes, then five more, and . . .

No, she told herself firmly, she was going to knock on that door, right that second.

She didn't move.

Oh, darn, she thought. She'd been so sure of herself up until this moment. After waiting for Steve and Mandy to return from Aspen she'd told Steve she needed Dutton's address in San Francisco and that she had no time to answer any of his questions. Steve had been so stunned by Bliss's uncharacteristic behavior that he'd scribbled the address on a piece of paper.

She didn't know exactly when she'd be back, she'd informed him, so they'd have to muddle through at Barton Property Management without her for now. Steve had bobbed his head up and down, said he'd tell their parents that she was off to the coast, then asked her if she'd been drinking champagne again.

"Oh, hush, Steve," Mandy had said. "Bliss is a woman in love who is going to her man. Quit being such a fuddy-duddy, Steve Barton."

"Indeed," Bliss had said, and swooshed out the door in a dramatic exit.

Now, there she was, hours later, after countless delays caused by airline arrangements that had been difficult to make because of the multitude of holiday travelers. There she was, with her suitcase in her hand and a cold knot of fear in her stomach, wondering what on earth had possessed her to do such an impulsive thing.

She was in love with Dutton McHugh. And she truly believed that he loved her.

That was why she was there, she thought, taking a deep, steadying breath. Her entire future happiness was behind the door she was staring at like an idiot.

But . . .

What if she was wrong? What if Dutton didn't really love her after all? What if he'd said all he had out of big-brotherly kindness and concern, not out of love? Oh, good Lord, she was going to make a complete fool of herself. What if Dutton wasn't even home because he was out with another woman, or there was a woman in there with him now?

Oh, mercy, what a stupid idea this had been.

No! she told herself. Mandy had been right. She was a woman in love who had come to her man. If Dutton didn't love her as she did him, he'd have to look her right in the eyes and tell her so. She'd accept that with dignity, then slink away and cry for the next fifteen years straight.

Oh, saints above, she wanted to go home.

No, no, no. She was knocking on that door right now. She did have the courage and fortitude to do this.

With rather detached fascination, Bliss saw her hand float up into the air, curl into a fist, and knock on the door. She jumped in surprise at the sound, then squared her shoulders. Her heart was beating wildly, the thudding cadence echoing in her ears.

Oh, Dutton, please, she silently begged. Please, please, please.

The door was opened and there he was.

Magnificent Dutton McHugh.

Dressed in faded jeans and a bright red sweater,

he stood in the doorway, causing her breath to catch and her knees to tremble.

"Bliss?" he said, then shook his head slightly. "Is it really you?"

"You betcha, McHugh," she said, waving her hand breezily in the air. A little, near-hysterical laugh escaped from her lips. She swallowed heavily, cleared her throat, and tried again. "What I mean is, yes, it's me. May I come in? I'd like to talk to you. Providing, of course, that this is a convenient time for you."

"Yes, yes, of course it is," he said. He gripped her arm and nearly hauled her off her feet and into the large living room of the obviously expensive apartment. He took her suitcase, closed the door, set the case on the floor, then placed her coat on a chair. His gaze swept quickly over the royal blue slacks and blue-and-white ski sweater she wore. "Bliss, I . . ."

She turned slightly and gasped. "Oh."

Standing in majestic beauty against the far wall was a huge, beautifully decorated Christmas tree. The lights were a brilliant rainbow, the shiny ornaments glittered brightly.

And on the top of the tree was a Christmas angel.

Bliss walked over to the tree, her gaze missing no lovely detail. She suddenly became aware that Christmas carols were playing on a stereo and a fire burned in the hearth. She turned to face Dutton, who was still standing by the door.

"The tree," he said quietly, "is artificial. There wasn't a decent one left on the lots when I got back here, so I had to settle for artificial. But only for this year, because I like live trees, and I know how to pick the best and—"

"Dutton?" she said, interrupting him.

"The tree, the carols, the fire," he went on. "I did it all for you, Bliss. I set it all up, and I've been waiting, hoping and praying you'd think through all I said that last night and come to me. I swear to God, I would have left that tree standing and kept a fire going through next July if that's how long it took. These past days and nights have been agony, not knowing what you were thinking, if you'd ever come, but I kept telling myself I had to give you time, be patient. Talk to me, Bliss, please. Tell me why you're here."

Tears misted her eyes, and her voice was shaky when she spoke. "Oh, Dutton, I was so confused. All of my life I've seen myself as a misfit within my own family. They loved me—I never doubted that—but I was different, didn't think or act like them. I wanted to fit in, tried to, and I was seeking their approval long past the age when it should have mattered or been so important."

Two tears slid down her cheeks, and she hastily brushed them away.

"Everything you said to me," she continued, "was true. I've been hiding behind my wall, convinced I was never going to be even close to becoming a real Barton. I didn't recognize the changes in myself as time passed because I'd closed my mind to the pos-

sibility it would ever happen. Black and white . . .
Yes, that's how I viewed things, just like you said. I
was fuddy-duddy Bliss. You were Steve's best friend,
a Barton-type man, out of my reach."

"Bliss . . ." He started toward her.

"No, please," she said, raising one hand to stop
him. "Let me finish." She took a deep breath and
fought against her tears. "Dutton, you were my
Christmas present, because I believed we were so
different, had so little in common, that you could be
mine only for a few stolen days. I told myself we
would create precious memories that would be
enough for me in the future. But the memories
wouldn't have been enough because I—I fell in love
with you."

He took another step toward her, but she shook
her head.

"Stay there, please. This is so difficult for me.
After you left, I cried. That's all I did, I just cried and
cried. Then I realized I had to get on with my life,
the tears had to stop. I started thinking about what
you had said to me, and suddenly it was clear, all of
it. The pieces to the puzzle fit at long last. Dutton,
I'm Bliss Barton. A Barton in some ways, but not in
others, just as you are. I'm a woman, complete within
myself, needing no one's approval but my own."

"Yes, that's right," he said, his voice raspy. "That's
what I was trying so desperately to make you understand."

"I asked myself why you had done that for me

and then left me on my own to figure it out. And I came to a conclusion that gave me the courage to come here. Now, as I see the Christmas tree, the fire, I pray I was right. Oh, Dutton, please tell me that I was right, that you love me as much as I love you." Tears spilled onto her cheeks again. "Do you love me, Dutton McHugh? Do you?"

With a moan that seemed to be torn from his soul, Dutton closed the distance between them and pulled her into his arms, holding her in a tight embrace. He buried his face in her fragrant hair as he strove to gather his emotions, then lifted his head to meet her gaze.

"Oh, yes my sweet Bliss, I love you. Leaving you that night was the most frightening thing I've ever done, but I had no choice. I ran the risk of losing you forever. I told myself that you loved me, but as each hour passed, I became even more afraid that maybe I'd been wrong. I waited for you, sweet Bliss, re-created our Christmas, and waited for my Christmas angel. And you came. Oh, thank God, you came."

His mouth melted over hers in a searing kiss. Their tongues met, and passions flared instantly. All the memories of doubts and pain, of loneliness and confusion, were hurled into oblivion, forever forgotten. There was only now, and the dreams of the tomorrows yet to come.

Dutton lifted his head. "I love you. Lord, how I love you. Marry me, Bliss. Please? Say you'll be my wife, my angel for every Christmas we'll share in the years ahead."

"Oh, yes, Dutton," she said, smiling at him. "I'll marry you. I love you more than I can ever begin to tell you. I'll have my Christmas present every day for the rest of my life."

He kissed her again. "There's a gift for you under the tree."

"For me? But I don't have anything for you. I was still trying to decide what to get you."

"I have what I want . . . my Christmas angel. Go ahead. Open it."

She moved out of his arms to pick up the small box, and quickly tore away the bright paper. As she removed the lid and brushed back the tissue, a soft sigh of pleasure whispered from her lips.

Attached to a gold chain was a delicate, exquisitely made charm.

An angel.

"Oh, Dutton, it's beautiful."

He took it from the box, fastened it around her neck, then turned her to face him again.

"Merry Christmas, my love," he said, and brushed his lips over hers.

"Merry Christmas, and Happy New Year, too."

"No, we're still concentrating on Christmas, because we weren't together on that day. We'll work our way up to New Year's."

"Oh? That's a lot of time to catch up on."

"So, I suggest we get started. I want to make love with you, sweet Bliss."

"Oh, Dutton McHugh, yes."

And there in front of the blazing fire, they were one, celebrating Christmas, their love, and their commitment to a lifetime together.

Later they dozed in the glow of the flames, the twinkling, rainbow lights of the tree showering them in a waterfall of color.

The gold charm nestled between Bliss's breasts seemed to shine brighter and brighter, as though possessing a special magic known only to the angels of Christmas . . . .

THE EDITOR'S CORNER

There is never a dull moment in our LOVESWEPT offices where we're forever discussing new ideas for the line. So, fair warning, get ready for the fruits of two of our brainstorms . . . which, of course, we hope you will love.

First, expect a fabulous *visual* surprise next month. We are going to reflect the brilliance of our LOVESWEPT author's romances by adding *shimmer* to our covers. Our gorgeous new look features metallic ink frames around our cover illustrations. We've also had a calligrapher devote his talent to reworking the LOVESWEPT lettering into a lacy script and it will be embossed in white on the top metallic border of the books. Each month has a color of its own. (Look for gleaming blue next month . . . for glimmering rosy red the following month.) So what will set apart the books in a given month? Well, the author's name, the book's title, and a tiny decorative border around the art panel will have its own special color. Just beautiful. We've worked long and hard on our new look, and we're popping with prideful enthusiasm for it. Special thanks go to our creative and tireless art director, Marva Martin.

Around here we believe that resting on laurels must be boring (could it also be painful?). And, like most women, all of us LOVESWEPT ladies, authors and editors, are out to prove something as time goes by—namely, *the older we get . . . the better we get . . . in every way!*

Our exciting news has taken so much space that I'm afraid I can give only brief descriptions of the wonderful romances we have coming your way next month. However, I'm sure that just the names of the authors will whet your appetite for the terrific love stories we have in our bright new packages.

Delightful Kay Hooper has come up with a real treat—not just one, but many—the first of which you'll get to sample next month. Kay is writing a number of LOVE-SWEPTs that are based on fairy tales . . . but bringing
(continued)

their themes completely (and excitingly!) up to date. Next month, *Once Upon a Time . . .* **GOLDEN THREADS,** LOVESWEPT #348, tells the love story of Lara Mason who, like Rapunzel, was isolated in a lonely, alien life . . . until Devon Shane came along to help her solve the problems that had driven her into hiding. An absolutely unforgettable romance!

In a book that's as much snappy fun as its title, Doris Parmett gives us **SASSY,** LOVESWEPT #349. Supermodel Sassy Shaw thought she was headed for a peaceful vacation in Nevada, but rancher Luke Cassidy had other plans for his gorgeous guest. This is a real sizzler . . . with lots of guffaws thrown in. We think you'll love it.

The thrilling conclusion of The Cherokee Trilogy arrives from Deborah Smith next month with **KAT'S TALE,** LOVESWEPT #350. Kat Gallatin, whom you've met briefly in the first two of the Cherokee books, is unorthodox . . . to say the least. She's also adorable and heartwarming, a real heroine. That's what Nathan Chatham thinks, too, as he gets involved with the wildcat he wants to see turn kitten in his arms. A fabulous conclusion to this wonderful trio of books—a must read!

Tami Hoag tugs at your heart in **STRAIGHT FROM THE HEART,** LOVESWEPT #351. Jace Cooper, an injured baseball star, was back in town, and Rebecca Bradshaw was desperate to avoid him—an impossibility since she was assigned to be his physical therapist. In this sizzler Rebecca and Jace have to work out the problems of a wild past full of misunderstanding. **STRAIGHT FROM THE HEART** is a sensual and emotional delight from talented Tami.

Patt Bucheister gives us another real charmer in **ELU-SIVE GYPSY,** LOVESWEPT #352. Rachel Hyatt is a Justice of the Peace who married Thorn Canon's aunt to some stranger . . . and he's furious when he first encounters her. But not for long. She makes his blood boil (not his temper) and thoroughly enchants him with her

(continued)

off-beat way of looking at the world. Don't miss this marvelous love story!

THE WITCHING TIME, LOVESWEPT #353, by Fayrene Preston is delicious, a true dessert of a romance, so we saved it for the end of LOVESWEPT's September feast. Something strange was going on in Hilary, Virginia. Noah Braxton felt it the second he arrived in town. He knew it when he encountered a golden-haired, blue-eyed witch named Rhiannon York who cast a spell on him. With his quaint aunts, Rhiannon's extraordinary cat, and a mysterious secret in town, Noah finds his romance with the incredible Rhiannon gets unbelievably, but delightfully, complex. A true confection of a romance that you can relish, knowing it doesn't have a single calorie in it to add to your waistline.

We hope you will enjoy our present to you of our new look next month. We want you to be proud of being seen reading a LOVESWEPT in public, and we think you will be with these beautifully packaged romances. Our goal was to give you prettier and more discreet covers with a touch of elegance. Let us know if you think we succeeded.

With every good wish,

Carolyn Nichols

Carolyn Nichols
Editor
LOVESWEPT
Bantam Books
666 Fifth Avenue
New York, NY 10103

BANTAM
SHOP·AT·HOME
C·A·T·A·L·O·G

Special Offer
Buy a Bantam Book
for only 50¢.

Now you can have Bantam's catalog filled with hundreds of titles plus take advantage of our unique and exciting bonus book offer. A special offer which gives you the opportunity to purchase a Bantam book for only 50¢. Here's how!

By ordering any five books at the regular price per order, you can also choose any other single book listed (up to a $5.95 value) for just 50¢. Some restrictions do apply, but for further details why not send for Bantam's catalog of titles today!

Just send us your name and address and we will send you a catalog!

THE DELANEY DYNASTY

Men and women whose loves and passions are so glorious it takes many great romance novels by three bestselling authors to tell their tempestuous stories.

THE SHAMROCK TRINITY

THE DELANEYS OF KILLAROO

Now Available!

THE DELANEYS: *The Untamed Years*